ALSO BY ASH LINGAM

To Hell and Back

I0609901

UNWANTED REUNION

UNWANTED REUNION

JED & JODIE DESPERADOS
BOOK 2

ASH LINGAM

WISE WOLF
BOOKS

WISE WOLF BOOKS
An Imprint of Wolfpack Publishing
wisewolfbooks.com
1707 E. Diana Street
Tampa, FL 33610

Paperback ISBN 978-1-965596-49-4
eBook ISBN 978-1-965596-48-7

This book is dedicated to my grandson, Kai.

"In a closed society where everybody's guilty, the only crime is getting caught. In a world of thieves, the only final sin is stupidity."

Hunter S. Thompson

UNWANTED REUNION

PREFACE

Even though Jodi Goodnight's uncle was the most famous rancher in Texas, it didn't save his niece from the law. When she unknowingly pistol-whipped a man who turned out to be the town sheriff, she had to go on the run. She deformed him for life, and he wanted revenge.

Jed Coal and John Noland rode under Quantrill's Raiders during the Civil War. John, because he was a slave and his owner forced him to take his place in the fighting so he could stay safe at home. And Jed, who was regular army, but was drafted by Quantrill himself due to his marksmanship qualities. Both men chose to do as they said or face a firing squad for disobeying a direct order.

The two ex-raiders and Jodi Goodnight escape and return to their little hideout a couple of days south of the Mexican border. Jodi is already planning their next heist. They intend to rob the casino aboard the Texas Belle, which ran out of Galveston, Texas.

The law wanted the three due to no initial wrongdoing of their own. They got forced into a life of crime, so they believed they might as well act accordingly. They had nothing to lose.

CHAPTER 1

STEAMSHIPS & CASINOS

As the paddle boat churned its way out of Galveston harbor, they could feel the deck move under their feet. They didn't know if the captain would turn back to port or carry on to the next stop to turn them over to the Army. From the look in his eyes, he was planning something first. Two men and a woman sat in straight-back chairs. Blood pooled under the White man's boot.

The steamship captain of the Texas Belle was tall with dark-brown hair—like Jed's—but with pale cruel eyes and ten years older. Over his temples and ears grew traces of gray.

"The least you can do is let the woman go!" Jed spat. "She didn't have a damned thing to do with Quantrill's Raiders or the Missouri Marauders. She ain't wanted by the Army. I doubt she's ever left Texas, and she sure as hell ain't been in Missouri. John and I admit our guilt— you caught us dead to rights. But ya gotta let the woman go."

Jed paused to let his words sink in. Then he added,

"I'd go easy if I were you. Her uncle's a powerful man here in Texas."

That got him a quick backhand across the cheekbone with the barrel of a Navy Colt. It was Jodi's pistol. Jed felt the pain, but he didn't care. He'd lived real agony in the war. Sometimes pain was a good thing. It meant he was still alive; most times, it just made him meaner.

Jodi's bright blue eyes flashed both fear and anger—both things she felt. They all three sat on chairs in a ship's cabin with their hands tied before them. It was hard to believe a random sailor recognized the two marauders from the fliers posted across Missouri and Kansas. Then again, a Black man and a White man traveling together with money stood out like a fox in a henhouse. However, the last thing they wanted was to get Jodi mixed up in all the Missouri-Kansas war business.

Many said it was the bloodiest part of the war, especially since the Lawrence Massacre on August 21, 1863. John and Jed were both there that day with Captain Quantrill and Bloody Bill Anderson. They had their orders and were left no choice. It made the pair of ex-raiders two of the most wanted men in Texas, as well as the country.

Blood leaked from a hole in the leg of Jed's pants, but he ignored the wound left by the skipper's knife. The captain shot around the table and kicked the chair out from under him. Jed flopped on the floor like a caught fish. The captain still held the blade in one hand and Jodi's pistol in the other.

Jed and John knew the captain wouldn't kill them because the bounty for their capture was too large. Lucky for the Rebels, the Yankees wanted them alive.

UNWANTED REUNION 3

Probably to make a show of their hangings, justice served for the public and the newspapers. A public hanging would make many people money in the news world and provide others power politically. Neither man was sure what this salty dog would do with Jodi were they to be left alone.

When the cabins' porthole shattered, they looked toward the window, but the image of a man had just disappeared. When they turned back, they saw the captain on the floor with a hole in his gut. His stomach wound was pumping blood onto the deck, obviously too much and too fast. Jed grabbed his knife, cut his bindings, and seized Jodi's Navy Colt as he hid behind the door. It wasn't two seconds later when a man with two pistols rushed into the room. Jed didn't hesitate. He pulled the trigger once—then again to make sure the man was disabled.

The shooter dropped to the floor. He was still alive because Jed didn't want him dead just yet. He was wide-eyed and trembling. His finger was still on the trigger of his pistol. Jed stepped on his wrist and pulled the gun out of his hand. He was in bad shape. A million questions shot through their minds. Was this a bounty hunter looking to get the reward, or was he one of Captain Quantrill's diehard raiders?

He was the second man to spot them on the ship, and they weren't two miles outside of Port Galveston. Getting aboard a riverboat looked like it wasn't the best of choices. Maybe they should have started with a train.

"Who sent ya?" Jed asked, hobbling toward the man he shot. "Or did ya come all on your own?" His wounded leg caused him to limp.

One of the Texas Belle crewmembers had pointed

them out to the captain, and he surprised all three with a half dozen sailors with guns. The captain immediately stabbed Jed in the leg to hinder his movement were he to try to escape. He apparently considered Jed the biggest threat and wasn't taking any chances.

However, he didn't expect much from the Black man or the whore who accompanied them. Claret seeped into Jed's boot. He wasn't sure the shooter could hear him or not. Whoever the man was, he didn't act scared. His eyes spread so wide they looked like they would pop out of his head, not from fear but pain. When he tried to swallow, foamy blood poured from his lips. A pool was forming under his body.

The shooter's breath hitched, and he grabbed Jed's pant leg tight before everything went limp. He died without giving them any information about who he was or who sent him. They didn't get anything to help them discover who else was on their trial. Jed and John quickly rifled his pockets.

They ransacked his clothing like that did on those dark nights on the killing fields. In seconds they checked him thoroughly, and the only clue they found was another copy of the flier. It was another wanted poster with pictures of John Noland and Jed Coal. They were sketches. The likeness for John was remarkable, but Jed's looked a bit like Jesse James with a beard. They looked at each other. The bounty was still the same, and it said, *WANTED ALIVE: $1,000 REWARD* for information leading to the capture of Jed Coal and John Noland. The sketches left little to the imagination.

"I doubt he be from the Missouri Raiders," Jed said. "They won't come after us for the money. It would more likely be revenge."

Jed was too confused to know the truth. Maybe he was lying to himself.

"We best run for it. You're gonna have to stay behind, Jodi. You'll hide better on your own," Jed said. "It's just too dangerous. Maybe we can meet up later down south if we get that far. You can still flee. We're close to shore. You can make a swim to freedom. It's your last chance, darlin'."

Still bound, Jodi looked at him with amazement. He called her "darlin'." Jed's words of endearment always came at her when she least expected it. There was no way she was going to go anywhere.

"Are you going to cut me loose or not?" Jodi spat spitefully.

Angry, her face turned the color of a turnip. Once she was free, Jodi got up enraged and slapped both men's faces. Then she hugged them, her emotions running wild.

"I ain't leaving, Jed," she said as her eyes teared up. "I'm not one to leave a chore half done. We still ain't robbed the casino."

There were the briefest moments of surprise on Jed and John's faces—but only a moment. Both men were cool under fire. So was Jodi, to a point. She always bucked up to what lay ahead. Her determination was evident, and they were already aware of her willpower.

They shrugged their shoulders and gave up arguing. There was no more time. It was clear the strong-headed woman wouldn't change her mind despite the sudden bloodshed. It was becoming far too commonplace for Jed and John. They had hoped to leave all this behind when they ran from the war, but it appeared their battles were far from over. Trouble seemed to follow them wherever they went.

"Get the keys from the captain," Jed said to John. "He locked our guns in that locker. I don't know who this fool thought he was playing with. He obviously thought himself something special."

"You ain't so special now, are ya?" Jed growled at the dead men. "Quick, before the ship's crew comes looking for the skipper. It looks like nobody heard the gunshot, but let's get out of here just the same."

"What about the man who recognized us?" John asked. "He's dangerous to us now."

The captain's eyes were already blank, as were the shooters. They weren't sure how many men were after them.

"I reckon robbin' the casino won't matter much, now," John said. "Not with the mess we've managed to get ourselves into in a couple of hours. We have little more to lose."

"What's the plan?" Jed asked Jodi as he and John waited. She always seemed to have a plan.

"What plan?" Jodi replied. "Once you two got recognized, our plans went right out the window. Plans only work when you've got the element of surprise."

Then she thought for a moment and said, "Since they've already recognized us, why not just rob the place? Bust right in with guns a blazin.' Ain't that what your friends would do?"

"Which friends?" Jed asked.

"Jesse and Frank James." Jodi smiled.

"I don't know if I'd call the James brothers friends?" John replied. He always felt he had to keep an eye on Jesse, but maybe it was just him being

Black and Jesse being so fervent for the southern cause.

"They ain't ever done us any harm," Jed said. Most people couldn't help but like Frank and Jesse. Of course, Jesse was Jesse. There was nobody else like him, so it was hard to compare.

Jed pulled his hat down low to hide his face the best he could, and Jodi quickly wrapped her hair in a knot on the top of her head. When she put her hat back on, she looked like another cowgirl.

"I'll go find the sailor who pointed us out," John said, then turned and slipped out the door. "I'll meet y'all in the casino."

Jodi went to say something, but Jed gave her a stare that shut her up. She had convinced them to spare people too many times, and it nearly cost them their lives on each occasion. Now, they were going to do things their way. Both Jed and John had years of experience at war and had managed to stay alive. That was no small feat, especially when riding with Quantrill's bunch. Jodi relented. She felt it was time to let them run the show and learn from experienced guerrillas for a change. She was the planner, but they were the facilitators.

Jed stood by the doorjamb with his back to the wall. Jodi was right behind him. When they saw no one outside, they darted out and down three flights of stairs. Then they casually crossed the ship's length and up, two more flights of steep steps to the casino. They could hear the noisy crowd from two decks down. Suddenly they were in a room with colored lights. A roulette wheel was the centerpiece of the room. Along one wall was a wheel of fortune. All the numbers had brightly colored backgrounds. The lever clicked loudly as the wheel spun around until it stopped on a lucky number. A roar reverberated through the crowded room.

A shole in the crowd won the prize, which he would return to the owner after the night was over. There was little control on the gambling on steamboats and even less law. In theory, the captain was the man in charge of everything that happened on the vessel. With him dead, the trio had to look out for his first mate. He would be the second-in-command.

Jed stepped over to Jodi and asked, "How in the hell are we supposed to rob a place with so many people? We could rob one side of the casino and the other side not even know it." He was so close he smelled the lavender soap she used to wash.

They made their way to the five blackjack tables, which stood in a row beside the entrance. They discreetly played their hands for small stakes as they killed time and waited for John to appear. It seemed to be taking too long, and Jed was getting edgy. The commotion in the room added to the tension. You could almost feel the gambling fever vibrate in the air. Everything smelled of money.

Since the war, Jed didn't like being in small rooms with thick crowds of people. The gambling hall was shoulder-to-shoulder with gamblers, and he was sweating bullets.

It reminded him too much of the days when they battled on horseback and on foot against impossible odds. Then too, there were masses of humanity, but they were all trying to survive, not win a few coins. When they lost, it wasn't monetary. It was their lives.

CHAPTER 2

LULLABY

JOHN TRACKED MEN FOR A LIVING FOR NEARLY SEVEN years during his time in the war. His owner loaned him to the cause in Missouri early on. There was trouble on the border with Kansas for a few years before that. His brave owner surrendered the services of his most trusted slave to the Confederate army. Of course, Mr. Noland didn't participate as he felt himself above such things as war and death. So Jed got thrown into the midst of the most infamous of all the Rebel companies—Quantrill's Raiders.

He became Captain William Quantrill's personal scout and was soon considered irreplaceable. The captain always kept him close to do specific jobs across enemy lines. He had many years to hone his killing skills. All this was before he started working as a sniper team with Jed Coal and why they both were wanted men.

John had never tracked a man on a riverboat before, though. How to strike and get away was going to be the stickler. All three of them could swim, depending upon how far they were from shore. With every moment, land was becoming more distant. Then again, before they could escape, they had to rob the casino. It dawned on John; he had never been in a casino. Enslaved people had no money for such luxuries, even if they were allowed entry—which they weren't.

The only gambling John ever did was to wager a penny on a game of checkers, which was only because he usually won. Occasionally, he had pitched pennies against the side of the shed in which they lived.

Shadows filled the corners and walkways on the paddleboat. It was darkest on the bow. There was a heavy fog in the bay, making it difficult to make out the moving shapes. He still didn't see the sailor. John quickly studied the stairs the deckhands frequented the most and stepped into a dark corner where he remained unseen to those passing by. If he were lucky, all the sailors would be busy with their tasks as the paddleboat got underway.

Blending into the darkness, John was impossible to see. When he bit off a piece of tobacco, his white teeth flashed in the dark as he calmly awaited his moment. Voices came and went, as did soldiers up and down the stairway. He was calm and patient. He felt the steady beat of his heart between his temples.

When the time came, John flicked his wrist and an ice pick dropped from his sleeve and into his hand. As the lone sailor passed and took his first step up the stairs, John grabbed him and put one hand over his mouth. With the other, he drove the icepick into the base of the man's head. He wiggled it around just enough to ensure fatal damage. When he slipped it out, he caught the body as his legs collapsed and helped him to the side of the boat. The paddle wheels drowned out the splash of his body, which quickly sank.

Next, John turned for the deck with the casino where Jed and Jodi were waiting. He needed more time. Soon they would be out to sea and too far from shore. Noise spilled out of the entrance of the casino along with the flash of colored light. John made his way up the steps as he wiped the ice pick clean and slipped it up his sleeve. When he walked into the room, he was so distracted he almost forgot what he was there to do. The lights, the colors, and the loud voices were overwhelming in both a good and a bad way. It was like something out of a fantastical dream. He felt a tug at his jacket and turned and saw Jed's emerald-green eyes. Behind him stood Jodi.

"What's the plan now with all these people?" John asked as he talked in Jed's ear.

A deafening rumble came from the patrons as someone won or lost at the wheel. People had to yell to be heard, and there must have been a hundred people in the casino. It was busting at the seams. A multitude of voices resonated over the room.

"Like Jesse James style," Jed replied.

"What?" John asked. The crowd was so loud he couldn't hear himself think. That and he was distracted by all the colorful lights and sounds. He never imagined a casino would be such a noisy place.

"JESSESE JAMES!" Jed yelled—louder than he intended.

Suddenly, the casino went quiet. Every damned person in the room stopped talking and turned toward Jed, John, and Jodi. They were an imposing sight.

All three were armed—the men heavily. Even the

woman had a pistol in her hand with the barrel aiming at the gamblers. The only word the crowd in the room heard was *Jesse James*. To the outlaws' surprise, everyone reached for the sky as soon as they heard the name.

At first, Jed and John were too shocked to react. It appeared Jesse was already making himself a reputation. Today, the gamblers thought Jed was the younger and most notorious of the James brothers.

"Pull your guns, fools," Jodi hissed as every eye in the room looked their way.

"All we want is the money from the tables," Jed announced, quickly coming to his senses. "All you honest folks, keep your cash. We'll make do with the Texas Belle's money. Fill up those bags, gentlemen."

Jed and John gave the man at the roulette table and the wheel of fortune each a sack and used another to clean out the house at the blackjack tables, where they had played earlier. It was almost comical how everybody cooperated. The latest stories of Jesse James must have become harrowing. Jed reminded himself to see what Jesse and his brother were up to.

All could see the menacing look in Jed's eyes. All the dealers and even the floor manager cooperated. Nobody put up any resistance at all. Each of the outlaws walked out of the floating casino with a bag full of money. They heard many hushed voices repeating the name of Jesse James as they left.

"Do you think they thought I looked like Frank?" John asked and started to laugh again.

"Now, what are we supposed to do?" Jed asked as he swung his revolver around behind them, but nobody was following.

"I can swim like a fish, but I doubt I float with this

bag full of money," John said. "Now that we've got the money, I don't fancy leaving it or giving it back."

"All boats have a tender," Jodi said as she grabbed their arms and raced for the ship's stern.

"What's a tender?" John asked as adrenaline roared through his body.

"It's a small boat used to go from anchorage to the docks or work on the hull. Usually, there's one in tow off the back of a boat. Lucky, this is a double-paddlewheel boat. Come on; we don't have much time before those folks get brave again or figure out, we ain't the James Gang."

Sure enough, there was a small rowboat floating on a mooring line behind the steamship, just like Jodi said. John pulled the line in hand over fist, and the three scrambled aboard. Jed grabbed the ores and dug them deep into the water, pulling them quickly away from danger with each powerful stroke.

Almost immediately, they vanished into the fog. They could only hear the splashing ores of the paddleboat until the dense fog consumed the sound. Finally, the only sound was a ship's bell somewhere and the faint sound of Jed dipping the ores in the water.

"Ain't that the damnedest thing you've ever seen?" John asked, laughing at his own humor. "I can see them mixing you up with Jesse James because of your eyes. But I hardly look like Frank James. Hell, I ain't even the right color."

John broke into another fit of laughter. He sure did laugh a lot lately. Then again, this was as much freedom he had had in his entire life. Jed and Jodi could not even comprehend how he felt. He sure did laugh a lot for a man with a price on his head ever since they deserted from Confederate army a month before the war ended.

At the time, they had no idea of when the war would end, but they felt it coming. Supplies were scarce, and bullets were being rationed. They also saw younger and younger boys, Union and Confederate, on the battle-fields. Boys barely big enough to hold a heavy revolver gave their lives for nothing.

They died because General Robert E. Lee refused defeat even though knowing it was over. That was a sign the end was near. If the Confederacy was to lose, they both knew they had to flee. You acquired a reputation if you rode with men like the James and Younger boys, Capt. Quantrill and Bloody Bill Anderson. It was something much darker and unforgivable for the losing side.

Atrocities were committed by the Union side, too. The victors won the right to record what happened from their point of view, though. Union atrocities went unpunished as the victors wallowed in the spoils of war and the power of superiority.

It seemed like they had been rowing forever. Jed's energy was waning, but he knew he couldn't stop until they hit land. Exhausted, John pushed him aside and took over. Jed had bleeding blisters on his hands. For men like him and John, frenzied flight was nothing new, though. They hoped they were going the right way in the dense fog. Occasionally a shadowy figure of what must have been the sun broke through the thick mist. It was the only thing they had to guide themselves.

When the boat's keel hit the beach, and they ran ashore, Jodi nearly flew from the boat and over the bow. She still hadn't gotten her sea legs, and the small rowboat bobbed around in the water like a cork.

"I wonder where we are?" Jodi asked.

Noland closed his eyes, sniffed the air and said, "There are people that way. I smell stagnant water, too."

"Then we best go the other way, shouldn't we?" Jodi asked.

"Not if we want horses," John replied.

"I want my Sandy back," Jodi said sadly.

She'd had the mare since it was a colt. She was born on her father's farm. She remembered the day because her father surprised her with the gift on her birthday.

The ex-soldiers were no longer attached to their horses, of course. They lost too many over the years in battle. They used them, then got a fresh one and battled on. Jodi liked riding a pony just as bright as her, and there was no other like Sandy. She knew her horse had her back just like she had hers.

Jodi said determinedly, "We have to figure out how to retrieve my horse. I have no intention to leave her behind."

"You do remember we just robbed the riverboat's casino, don't you?" John asked.

"I don't care what we did," Jodi retorted. "You two can go on if you want. I'm gonna follow that steamship and steal my horse back on the next stop. They won't know she's mine until they get to the end of the line. If y'all come along, you can get your horses back too. We won't have to steal any more animals."

"That's a lot of risk-taking for a few animals," John said. He always saw things in a practical way. It's why he was still alive.

"My Sandy ain't just any animal. She's smarter than most men," Jody huffed. The men got her point.

Jed surprised John, though, and immediately caved in.

"All right, we'll go with you. We were going to have to steal some horses anyway. At least these are ours and not some poor souls who can't afford to lose an animal. I just hope we don't get shot for our efforts."

"So, what's the plan?" John asked. "You do have a plan, don't ya?"

"We walk across the gangplank down the stairs to the stables. We mount our horses and ride for the docks without hesitating. If anybody tries to stop us, my Sandy will run 'em over. Remember when she ran for you, Jed?"

"Yeah, I thought I was gonna have to shoot her until you whistled," Jed replied. "I swear that horse be half dog."

"Come on, you two," Jodi said as she trudged through the sand until they got to the edge of the sea grapes all along the shore. They knew they couldn't penetrate the mangroves, but they could cut their way through the sea grapes. To make sure nobody knew where they wandered off to John, chopped a hole in the bottom of the small rowboat, and sunk it in deep water. Then he covered their tracks across in the sand. Once they got themselves into the dense vegetation, they knew no one could follow them.

John went to work on the sea grapes, clearing a path to a dirt road. They got their bearings and headed for the next stop for the Texas Belle. They hoped they could get there before it finished loading more cargo and passengers and continued south. They weren't going to make it if they had to go on foot, though.

CHAPTER 3

DESPERADOS

WHEN THEY MADE IT TO THE ROAD, THE ONLY TRAFFIC WAS donkey-drawn carts loaded with sugar cane and cotton. Oxen pulled them and were even slower than the three outlaws.

When they saw a large dust cloud heading in their direction, John got worried.

"A cloud of dust that big means lots of horses," John said as he frowned and watched the mass of dirt creep closer.

"And what if it's not the Army? We can't shoot at people until we know which side they are on," Jodi said.

"The Blue Coats will be coming in uniform. The bounty hunters could look like you or me. Who knows? I doubt they'd run in a bunch and make that much dust. Men who trade flesh for money are usually stingy and don't like to be generous with their earnings," John replied.

"I usually can tell wicked men by the look in their eyes," John whispered. "You can see it there before they die. But you become accustomed to the look. Don't you worry. I'll know if they be friend or foe."

When they saw what was causing the massive cloud of dust, it was the last thing they expected. It was a weather-worn stagecoach. One of the few remaining since trains began to move across the country every which way.

Jodi removed her hat and unpinned her hair, letting it fall to her shoulders. When the old fellow driving the team of horses saw the pretty woman, he stood on the foot brake and pulled the reins to slow the six-horse team to a walk.

The wizened old driver offered a toothless grin at the pretty woman and asked, "What's a woman like you doing out here on your own?"

Then he saw John and Jed walk up behind her. His smile disappeared, but he didn't frown. He didn't hide it when he assessed the two.

"What can I do for you folks?" the stagecoach driver asked as he finally got the horses to a stop.

The team of animals stomped from one foot to another in their impatience to get back moving. A shotgun guard sat beside the driver, as mute as a stump. He hardly noticed the folks stranded alongside the trail, but his thumb was on one of hammers of the double-barrel shotgun and his finger inside the trigger guard. A Winchester rifle was propped up beside the gray-haired driver. His hat hung down his back from the stampede string showing his unruly silver mass that stretched into sideburns and a beard.

"We're the only express stagecoach that runs from Galveston to Port Lavaca, the first stop with a major reload on the voyage," the drivers said. "We cater to the folks that missed the ship when it weighed anchor. I must admit, despite the fall of stages in the territory, we're as busy as bees every day of the week."

Their next stop was Port Lavaca. That was only a hundred forty miles. Along the coast of the Gulf of Mexico. The ship's progress would all depend on the weather and the fog.

"Do you think you can make good enough time to catch the ship at Port Lavaca?" Jodi asked, concerned for her horse.

The old stage driver cackled and cracked the whip over the heads of the six horses. They got nervous and stirred, anxious to get going again.

"Don't you worry about a thing, ma'am," the driver said through a toothless mouth. He gummed a cheroot. "I've yet to let the steamship beat my rig. Ya, see, snags and branches don't hinder my progress, not to mention the fog. And if there's heavy rain, the paddleboat could be stranded for a day or more. Don't you worry that pretty little head of yours. We'll get y'all there in time to catch the Texas Belle south."

"I'm Mrs. Jodi Wilson, and this is my husband, Jed. This here is Mr. John Washington. We are all friends, but due to delays, we too missed the departure of the Texas Belle."

"It happens every day, ma'am. It keeps me in a job. July here too. He ain't much at talking, but he's as slick as spit with a shotgun and a rifle. Most folks call me Colorado Pete. The hell if I know why because my name is James, and I come to Montana. But it's stuck now, so y'all can call me whichever one ya want."

"How long does it take to get to Lavaca?" John asked.

"If we don't run into trouble, two days. But you're

going to have to hold on to your hats as I hardly stop and never slow down. It may be bumpy, but it'll be quick. Plus, it's the only way to get to the port before the Texas Belle loads and departs. Those ship's captains don't mess around once they get the cargo stowed."

The stagecoach driver didn't know that the ship's captain was dead. So, of course, there would be a certain amount of commotion on the docks resulting in an extended delay. They needed to get there before it arrived. Then nobody on the docks will know what happened, especially with the casino robbery. The three riders climbed aboard the stagecoach. Jed and Jodi were in the carriage, and John with the other colored folks was on the coach's roof. There was a cushioned seat on the very back of the wagon where two salesmen sat. It was the cheapest transport because you had to swallow a lot of dust.

Black men were free, but that didn't mean they got equal treatment. John only agreed to sit on the top with the other man of color because they didn't want to draw any more attention to themselves, especially as they were to return to the scene of their crime.

John knew he would never get even with all the White folks who had treated him poorly in the past. It was just the way things were. Jed and Jodi didn't like it either, but they couldn't afford to make a fuss now that they decided to save Jodi's horse, which was aboard the Texas Belle.

The ride was a nightmare. They stopped periodically to change horses, but they drove all night. The shogun guard and the driver took turns in between. The passengers all held on with white-knuckles. They felt like they had gone a few rounds with a boxer by the end of the second day. When Colorado Pete said two days, he meant it. They pulled up to Port Lavaca the next afternoon, and the Texas Belle had yet to arrive.

"Are y'all headed right back?" John asked as he climbed down from the top of the coach. Dirt covered him just like the driver and the man riding shotgun.

"Lord no," Colorado Pete said. "Another team of horses and drivers with do the return trip so we can rest. By the time the coach gets back, we'll have had four days off; then it's forty-eight hours straight again. It suits me fine, though. Half the time, I live like a bachelor, and the other, I let my wife boss me around. Here in Lavaca, July and I enjoy life away from our wives. Peace and quiet are what I want right now; that and a soft bed. It was a pleasure meetin' you folks. I wish y'all a pleasant cruise."

The stage driver climbed back aboard the coach along with July, released the set on the brake lever, slapped the trace reins across the animals' backs and headed for the stable and some food and rest.

As suspected, the situation at the docks was already chaotic, and the Texas Belle hadn't even arrived yet. Lines of people were waiting to get on board. There appeared to be some semblance of a line, but it was hard to tell. There must have been a hundred people jockeying for a better position to scurry aboard once the Texas Belle docked.

"We'll have to make our way on board and create some confusion so we can make our break amid the panic," Jodi said. "Once the local sheriff arrives and they hear Jesse James might be on the paddleboat, there probably will be a run for the exits. At least by the folks in the casino. There's no way for them to know the robbers didn't hide somewhere to get off the boat upon arrival in

Lavaca. I doubt any crew members dared search the ship as they already found their captain dead along with another unidentified man. None of them want to be the sailors who finds Jesse James. It would probably mean their deaths."

"That's the dumbest idea I've ever heard," John Noland grumbled. "It's so stupid it just might work. How do we get on board with all those people, though?"

"How many horses were there below decks, Jodi?" Jed asked as a plan began to form in his mind. "It may just work, especially if we create a stampede."

"It's hard to say," she replied. "There be goats, horses, sheep, longhorns, pigs, and even a few hundred chickens. I heard a donkey or two bray, too.

"Why?" John asked. "Whatcha thinking?"

A blast suddenly came from the whistle of the Texas Belle. Much to the outlaw's dismay, it was sounding the S-O-S. Three short blasts—three long and three more short. It created more confusion on the dock, where Union soldiers tried to maintain order as the ship approached.

The hands scurried about the deck, preparing fenders to hang along the hull so it didn't damage it upon impact with the dock. They secured the mooring lines in seconds, with the bowlines over the cleats. A crane swung the gangplank from a large beam as it neared what was now a line of people waiting to board. There was twice as many people pushing and shoving to get off the paddleboat, creating more chaos. Everybody who saw the robbery was doing their best to get off the ship because they thought Jesse James was aboard.

Most of the passengers were ticketed to the end of the line. Some had booked a round-trip excursion so they could enjoy a week of gambling. Now, they all wanted off the boat. The clash of passengers created immediate confusion on the docks. Even the deck hands, dressed in white, struggled in the crowd as fistfights broke out. Two men got shoved from the ramp to the pier and into the murky waters. None of them wanted to be shot by the famous Missouri outlaw.

"The mooring lines," Jed said as he turned and ran for the back of the ship where there was the least movement. John saw what he meant and raced for the stern of the paddleboat.

It appeared most of the first-class passengers poured down from the forward decks, and they now fought among themselves for the right to get off the boat first. There was such a funnel of people, nobody moved forward. It also impeded the ability of the military police to board. Nobody knew what was going on. The only thing they still heard was the name Jesse James repeated by guests and crew alike. His name created panic and terror.

As most of the crowd focused on the gangplank for the passengers to exit, without a word, Jed and John began climbing the mooring lines to the anchor's hawsepipe. They were large enough for a man to pass through with the mooring lines intact. Jed looked back, but Jodi was not a quarter of the way up the cable. Now they had no time, though. They scrambled up the thick hemp rope like a couple of water rats. They pushed themselves through the hawsepipe and onto the bow of the boat.

They had to get to the livestock on the bottom deck without anybody noticing. John easily mixed in the Black folks who rode the bottom decks and stables. They were free, but life didn't seem much different for them yet. It was actually getting harder. John believed the worst was yet to come before his people would reap the rewards they so long deserved.

As John and Jed pushed themselves into a dark shadow in the corridor's corner, John whispered, "I sure as hell hope that young filly is worth it."

Jed stopped in his tracks and asked, "What the hell do ya mean by that?"

"What you take me for, an old fool? I'd have to be blind not to see how she looks at you."

"This ain't the time or place, John. And this ain't about me."

"Ain't it? For you, there never is a time or place," John grumbled. "When we're out on the trail, if anybody says something you don't want to talk about, you ride off and disappear. Do you think I don't know all about you after four and a half years? Sometimes I think I know you better than you do. Stop pretending and running away from what you want, fool. Now, follow me. The servants' stairs are here in the back."

"The last thing I need now is a relationship and advice from a man who's never been married," Jed snapped, letting his anger slip and his voice sound harsher than he had wished. Jed wasn't the type to take things back, though.

"All right," John said. "If that's how ya want it. But one day, you're gonna realize what I say, and it will be too damned late to do anything about it. Most Black folks live a short life, and soldiers even shorter. I figure you, and I survived for some reason. If not, it was like we survived the war for nothing.

"Even I'm lookin' for more than just running till we

get caught. I fancy dreaming about a happy ending. It won't do ya a lick of harm. Everybody needs to believe in a little bit of hope."

"Are you ready to get this over or not? Or would you rather argue until the marshal finds us?" Jed retorted sarcastically. But John knew him well enough to know he listened to at least half of what he said.

John smiled that knowing smile and pulled a long, curved knife from his boot. James pulled a Bowie knife from the back of his belt and hidden under his jacket as they made their way down to the stables. All they had to do was smell their way. They took care climbing down the typically steep steps. The passengers from the lower decks wanted to get off the boat so badly; it was like they were running from the plague. Could they all be fleeing from who they thought was Jesse James? Hell, Jesses could get a scary look in his eye, Jed thought, but he was hardly the demon they made him out to be. Nobody even looked at John and Jed's faces as they raced down three decks.

Jed ran to the cattle loading hatch and began to hack at the thick lines that held the heavy timber door in place. It was supposed to fall outward, controlled by counterweights on the sides. There was no time for that now, though. As he labored cutting the eight-inch-thick hemp lines, John let every animal in the stables and live-stock pens loose. Pigs began screeching and running around frantically. It was absolute bedlam below decks when Jed finally cut through both lines, and the door came slamming down onto the floating dock. The entire ship rumbled on impact. Jed opened all the chicken cages, and birds ran and flew everywhere. It looked like Noah's Ark.

More screams came from the female first-class passengers. Suddenly hundreds of chickens, ducks, and geese began to scramble and fly for freedom. Then came the terrorized pigs. Some were so big they trampled spectators. A crowd scrambled to see what was happening on the Texas Belle. From behind sheep, goats, and cattle, Jed and John mounted and led a beige mare across the cattle landing gate. Jodi came running as soon as the two showed up with the horses. She ran toward Sandy and mounted her from the back, jumping and using her hands on her rump to guide her into the saddle. Again, they wheeled their horses south for the freedom in Mexico.

After riding for most of the day, they pulled up to rest and refresh the horses and themselves.

"Does anyone know what the hell happened back there?" Jodi asked as she snickered. "I'll bet they're still trying to figure it out."

"I doubt they think we be the James Gang anymore," John worried. "Not if anyone saw the three of us fleeing the scene. Hell, now we'll be wanted by the US Navy, too."

"The riverboats ain't part of the Navy," John replied.

"Yeah, but the river and the coastal waters are," Jed said. "We best get moving, stash the money from the casino, and head back to Mexico for a spell until things cool off."

CHAPTER 4

REVELATIONS

JODI HAD EVERY INTENTION OF HELPING THE BOYS retrieve their horses but found the thick mooring lines too big for her tiny hands. Jed and John climbed them easily. She barely made it back to the shore without slipping and falling into the harbor.

Immediately, she ducked into the shadows of a storage shed. When she turned, Jed and John had disappeared from sight. As she waited, she watched the arrival of the town constable and a marshal. Both had fliers in their hands and were trying to interview witnesses.

Fortunately, most women were frantic and half-hysterical from the scare. Few men were willing to divulge any information about the robbery. Most said they didn't see it because they turned their eyes to the ground. Others claimed they were on the other side of the room and didn't even notice the theft. A few went as far as to claim they didn't even know who Jesse James was.

Only the women attempted to give descriptions, but they varied from a red devil with horns and a tail to a desperado with trident and red eyes. All the women identified the photograph, but none seemed to remember seeing a White woman or a Black man.

It was the blackjack dealers who identified them. All three were busy at the tables when someone in the crowd called out Jesse James. They dove for cover as soon as they heard the outlaw's name. All three were positive they could identify the White woman and Black man if someone could find a picture of them.

The men in the crowd were a mix of southern supporters who thought what Quantrill and his men did to be heroic. Some thought the James brothers were heroes of the South, too. The other half were afraid of the repercussions if they spoke about such violent outlaws. The investigation turned into an immediate quagmire.

When there was a sudden crashing sound, the entire floating dock shuttered and bobbed in the water under the sheer weight of the ship's cattle ramp. It appeared the counterbalance failed, and it came thundering open. Immediately after came hundreds of chickens doing their best to gain flight or run for freedom. Following them were ducks and geese. The entire crowd stopped what they were doing to gawk and stare. Squealing pigs came next, ahead of two riders who picked their way down the cattle gangplank. It was clear they provoked the stampede by shooting several rounds into the air. That sent half the people diving face first for the pier.

The marshal looked from the poster and back to Jed as he fled from the paddleboat and said, "That don't look like Jesse James to me. And who in the hell is the Black fella? And where is his brother, Frank?"

"All I know is somebody yelled Jesse James and the

whole room went quiet," the blackjack dealer replied. "I ain't even sure who said it. The casino gets a mite noisy once things get going."

"Where's the rest of them wanted posters?" the marshal asked his deputy, who looked at him dumb-founded and shook his head.

"What are ya waitin' on? Go get 'em while the faces are still fresh in our memories," his boss said. "I bet a dime to a dollar the White fella be wanted for sure and maybe the Black fella too."

"What about the White girl?" one of the sailors asked.

"What White girl is this?"

"She was waiting on the two outlaws that rode down the cattle ramp with the horses. She jumped on the small beige mare," the sailor explained.

"Are you still here?" the marshal growled at his deputy, who was listening intently. "Get me those wanted posters to see who they be wanted by and why. One of you soldiers get an officer over here too. The James boys were with Quantrill, so the Army be the best to run 'em down."

"I don't fancy chasing Jesse James," the deputy said. His Adam's apple bobbing as he swallowed, hard. Beads of sweat rose on his brow.

After another sharp look from the lawman, the deputy turned and took off for the marshal's office and the stack of wanted posters. It was getting so they had so many fliers on outlaws they didn't know what to do with them all. Ever since the end of the war, wanted posters arrived in an endless stream. The marshal shifted through them the best he could, but there were just too many to remember.

Many of them were men wanted by the Union army,

either for desertion or for what they considered war crimes. As far as the marshal had seen, there was little humanity on either side. As a US Marshal, Charlie Coins didn't have to take up arms with the Confederacy. He and the Texas Rangers were needed to keep the peace along the border more than on the battlefield. Comanche and Mexican bandits tried to take advantage of the situation, what with most able-bodied Americans engaged in the Civil War.

Jesse James was a different matter. The reward for the James brothers was in the thousands of dollars now; it would take a brave or lucky man to collect that bounty. Marshal Coins knew he wasn't up to the task. He believed it was a case of mistaken identity. He'd heard they were in Kansas robbing banks not a week ago. Although, Quantrill's Raiders were known to winter in Texas.

When the marshal saw the cattle deck ramp drop and what looked like hundreds of chickens burst from the ship's hold, followed by every animal imaginable, he was startled. He stood like most, with mouth agape. Immediately, it dawned on him what was happening. It was the getaway. The outlaws must have hidden in cargo bay until the Belle docked. Marshal Coins was positive neither of the escapees were Jesse James. He had the James' posters nailed to the wall behind his desk. Jesse and Frank were two of the most wanted men in the West.

It wasn't long before the crowd quadrupled. As the people piled onto the floating dock—half of them curiosity seekers—it sank deeper. Soon they'd all be ankle-deep in water. Finally, the deputy arrived with the posters the marshal requested. He had to push his way up the gangplank.

"The first thing we need to do is look at the murdered captain and the other man who was killed," Coin explained to the first mate. "Does anybody have any idea of how it happened?" he asked.

There were a dozen interpretations, as usual with police work, but nobody actually had a clue. The lawman was certain somebody had shot through the porthole. Three chairs, with bindings still attached, confused the marshal's investigation. One of the chairs had dried blood on it.

Coins sat down and closed his eyes for a moment, attempting to reenact the murder that could have occurred a couple of different ways. The man shot twice could have broken in and shot the captain, but who fired the bullet from outside? And who was tied to the chairs? The blood-stain on made it obvious someone was wounded.

"Maybe one of the bullets ricocheted and broke out the window," the deputy said.

"Then the glass would be on the outside," Marshal Coins replied. "That's what makes this odd. I suspect there be more than just a casino robbery here. It just doesn't make any sense."

When the deputy finally came with the stack of wanted posters, a snooty Army lieutenant accompanied him. Marshal Coins had his share of dealings with the Army and intended to send this job his way if he could. He'd be damned if he'd traipse across the country to hunt the likes of Jesse James or someone like him. These men weren't just regular outlaws; they were professional killers with years of experience.

The investigators had spent the better part of an hour examining the scene and the wanted posters. Finally, Coin flipped to a wanted poster of two Confederates outlaws, one White and one Black. The flier explained both worked as snipers for Quantrill's Raiders and Bloody Bill's Marauders.

"Lookee here," Marshal Coin said. "A Corporal Jed Coal and a slave by the name of John Noland. They both be wanted for riding with Quantrill's Raiders. Don't that strike ya odd? The Black fella fighting for the South with the marauders. There's too much here we don't see yet. That's the White fella I saw riding off the boat, and that was the Black fella with 'em," Coin proclaimed, showing the wanted poster to the soldier.

"The Army wants these men for war crimes," Lieutenant Ira Moore said. "This will be my responsibility, Coins. This is a military matter now. Sergeant, get a patrol organized at once. We will meet back here in one hour. Is that understood?"

"Yes, sir, Lieutenant Moore," Sergeant Jim Johnson replied with a crisp salute. He turned and ran for his horse.

The lieutenant rode a massive horse to carry his size. He was a monster of a man on a monster of a horse.

The crowd still hadn't thinned out entirely by the time Sgt. Johnson returned with his cavalry patrol. They were ready to pursue the wanted ex-Confederate soldiers. As they rode out of Port Lavaca, a black flag appeared among the riders, a bad sign for the three on the run. A dozen riders followed their leader. Half of the men were war veterans, the others—enthusiastic recruits. You could easily distinguish one group from the other. Some bore visible wounds, and the determined eyes of men who had experienced the killing fields.

The recruits were the other side of the coin. They were too late for the Civil War or too far away from the action to participate. Their hearts were filled with vengeance for a war in which they never participated.

Marshal Coin was still scratching his head when they rode away, wondering what really happened aboard that steamship. Things just didn't tally up.

CHAPTER 5

NIGHTMARES

JOHN, JED, AND JODI PUSHED HARD UNTIL THEY PASSED THE Rio Grande and—in case the Army boys got feisty and forgot where America ended—maintained their pace for another day beyond the border. They were only one day from their little Mexican hideaway. This time they brought the stolen cash with them. They didn't dare stash it with the rest when every marshal and soldier in Texas was looking for them. Luckily for them, Texas was so vast it was like finding a flea on a large, hairy dog. They had run their horses hard, and now they wanted to give them a rest, so they hobbled them and let them nibble at the green grass beside a spring.

They had found the water hole by chance, and always stopped there on their way to El Molino, the Mexican village they've adopted for their hideout. The next day, they would ride into the little town, where they would rest for a week or two.

Most outlaws hide in hard-to-find places. These three chose to hide in plain sight because they were free and not wanted in Mexico. They made sure their money got around, so everyone in the village profited. They were never got out of line with the town's citizens and even paid for a new roof for the town hall because the village coffers were empty. They were on a first-name basis with almost all one hundred inhabitants. They were simple people who wished for little, so they wanted for nothing. All they asked for was a decent meal and peace, much like the three, weary desperados.

For two nights, Jed had been plagued by nightmares from the Lawrence massacre. As a result. Jodi hardly got a blink of sleep. His undecipherable cries out were like a knife in her heart. The entire day after his nightmares, it was as if Jed was in a fog or haze. He stumbled around the camp listlessly.

John didn't dare travel when Jed was in this state of mind; if they had to fight, who knows what might happen. Even though they were close to El Molino, they stayed by the spring and kept Jed in the shade. If the nightmares provoked Jed to violence, it was best to stay out of town until the torture passed.

Jodi read a lot and knew all about Bloody Kansas. They say a hundred and fifty men and boys died the day of the Lawrence massacre. It must have been a horrific sight for all involved, especially for her two compatriots. She quickly understood how the war shaped them both. Of course, they could have refused to participate in the holocaust, but they would have been shot as traitors for disobeying orders. That was no choice at all, though. The war transformed young men into adult soldiers, regardless of age. The armies on both sides of the Mason-Dixon Line were losing veteran fighters so fast they could only replace them with inexperienced boys.

As they remained camped at the spring for the third

night, John Noland decided it was time for reconnaissance of the area. He wanted to make sure no army patrols or bounty hunters had located them. If he could find their pursuers first, they had the opportunity to bushwhack them on their way down the same trail. It was a tactic they used as a sniper team throughout the Civil War.

Jed finally was sleeping peacefully. He lay on his side with his head resting in his worn saddle and wrapped in a dark gray blanket. There was a chill in the air. So, when Jodi rose from her bedroll, she wrapped herself in her blanket. She tiptoed in her bare feet toward the sleeping soldier and lay down beside him. She sensed a calmness in his breathing.

Jed's dreams quickly came alive, emerging from a dark haze. They weren't nightmares anymore. The scent of fresh wildflowers and honey bombarded his senses as he felt her hot breath on his neck. Quickly, his dream blended into reality.

Jodi's heart thundered against her ribs and jumped into her throat. She was scared and excited at the same time. She whispered sweet nothings into his ear.

The tone of Jodi's voice, filled with emotion, lifted Jed from his dream state. He suddenly became alert. He didn't say a word because he felt silence was best as she nestled close to him. He opened his eyes and let his fingers weave through her thick hair and push it from her face. He stared into her eyes. They were blue and as big as the sky.

She moved her hand to his torso, searching. She cleared her throat, trying to ease some of the fear from her words, and asked, "Is it all right?" Again, the tremor of uncertainty was in her voice.

Shades of red and orange streaked the sky as the sun lay just under the horizon. A full moon broke out over the west and cast a magical glow over the campsite. They could hear the insects talking in the darkness. Somewhere bullfrogs croaked.

Jodi got close enough to Jed to smell his scent. It was like leather and smoke, mixed with an aura of musk.

Jed thought her face was iridescent in the moonglow. He ran his fingers on her bare arms, and her skin seemed hot to his touch. His face glistened with perspiration. A burning desire boiled deep within his core. It was impossible to contain.

Jodi was so excited the earth beneath her body seemed to disappear. Her heart raced and her palms became sweaty. She welcomed his need, surrendering her heart and body.

She marveled at how one so quick to violence could be such a gentle lover. He made her body tingle as she joined him.

When it was over, Jed seemed to fall into a deep sleep, finally at peace at the bottom of a still, dark well. How he could be so alive and awake one moment and sound asleep the next, she couldn't understand. She snuggled close to him, pulled his hand to her lips and kissed his fingers. His free hand rested on her waist as she drew the other to her bosom and closed her eyes in blissful contentment.

Still, arrows of disappointment prickled at her heart. This would have been the time to talk and ask long-pondered questions. Obviously, the answers were not coming anytime soon.

Maybe it's just as well. He might not be ready to offer the words I long to hear.

She knew deep down he cared but couldn't figure out why he showed it only on rare occasions, times when his defenses were down and his resistance low.

"I love you," she whispered in his ear, her voice trembling subtly because the man tangled her emotions. Even though she knew he was asleep, she saw his lips twitch into a slight smile. She fell asleep wishing he would speak the words his heart protected.

WHEN JED WOKE UP, Jodi and John were sitting by the fire pouring the day's first coffee. The aroma enveloped the clearing. Somewhere, far away, a rooster crowd. At first, Jed acted like he was still asleep. He didn't know when John returned and wondered if he knew about Jodi and him. Then again, John had mentioned, in passing, he had noticed they were developing a relationship.

He wasn't one to oversleep. So, he threw his blanket off, pulled a revolver from under his saddle, and pushed it down into his belt. Jodi didn't believe she ever saw Jed or John a foot or two from their Colt Walkers, and their rifles were never more than a couple of steps away.

"I reckon it was a good thing we went south with that Army patrol after us," Jed said, making sure the morning's discussion remained on their pursuers instead of romance.

Suddenly he looked warmly at his two partners and said, "I thank ya kindly. The demons get the best of me at times, and I ain't much good company. It's funny how I never remember much about them—but I know what they are and from where they come. I reckon one day they'll stop."

Shocked by his words, Jodi wondered if he remembered their lovemaking. Doubt creeped into her heart, creating anxiety. He was still under that strange spell created by the horrors of war. She longed to soothe his conscience so he could find peace. Then, he would fall in love with her.

"What's for breakfast?" Jed asked as he peeked into the pot. Steam covered his head, and Jed thumped his hand with his wooden spoon.

"The same damned thing we had yesterday and the day before," John grumbled. "If it weren't for you, we'd already be feasting on tortillas and tamales. I would have never imagined I'd like Mexican food so much. I could eat a whole quesadilla right now."

Jed tried to scoop a spoonful to get a taste.

"Wait like the rest of us," John said sternly. He was grumpy and putting on a show. "This morning, you're going to have to do with more salted pork and beans. There are some fresh frying-pan biscuits there if you want. That should hold ya over for another ten minutes. If not, then wait patiently like Jodi here."

Jodi saw the concern in the old Black man's eyes. He knew Jed better than anyone, and only he knew what he was capable of doing. Jodi hoped she never found out herself. He sure did have a passel of demons inside tormenting him. She wondered if he would ever heal enough for them to have a real relationship. She could tell he cared for her but believed himself to be damaged goods, refuse from a war that lasted far too long. He felt his time would soon come. It was a hell of a way to look to the future, but Jodi knew it to be the truth, as grim as it was.

She, too, knew her life would be considerably shorter

unless they were smart enough to make a big robbery, get away with the money and live somewhere safe. So far, they'd been too lucky.

In the first robbery, the bankers almost gave them their money. The second heist failed because of Jed and John's greed, but she believed they'd learned their lesson. She had to figure out how to make a robbery so big they would make every paper in the country. The trick was to commit the robbery without being identified. What fun was it if everybody knew who they were? Then there would be no future at all.

She couldn't help but dream John, Jed, and she could someday live like ordinary people. So far, their lives regularly had cast them to the wolves. She was tired of having them snapping at their heels. Jodi thought it was time to turn the tables.

CHAPTER 6

LOCOMOTIVES

TWO DAYS LATER, THE THREE OUTLAWS SAT ON THE tavern's porch at the edge of the village of El Molino. The name *Cantena Serena* stood out on the side in large, whitewashed letters. Jodi was learning everything she could from everyone around her. Nothing was beyond her comprehension; she even soaked up the Spanish language like a sponge. An old leather smith was teaching her how to braid bullwhips and use one. She seemed curious about everything she did.

"Do you two know what El Molino means?" she asked as they sat on the porch and relaxed. "It means windmill. That's what that old building was in the middle of town, but most of it has fallen apart with time. The folk from other farms would bring their grain corn here to grind it into meal."

"What does the Cantina Serena mean?" John asked.

"Serene Tavern," Jodi replied.

John smiled and said, "That sounds about right."

Although both men still carried their guns, they all had let their guards down. The locals felt the three gringos brought them good fortune by making the village their home away from home. None of them knew for sure they were outlaws, although they suspected as much. It was hard knowing what was right and what was wrong since the end of the Civil War. They knew there was much violence on the Mexican border as the Confederate fugitives ran south for safety. Many others ran for New Mexico and Arizona, places with fewer people and fewer laws. However, the area was rife with Apache.

John and Jed both loosened their gun belts after the meal. They didn't know half of what they ate, but it sure did taste good. Jed acquired a particular taste for jalapeño chili peppers.

They had been in El Molino for a week, and still, Jodi waited for Jed to come and visit her room. She was tired of having to take the initiative. It was his turn to show her how he felt. Sometimes she felt like he didn't even know she existed. Still, she knew he cared for her in his strange way, but he seemed afraid to think about the future. He felt their fate sealed, and there would be no heading back. It was almost like Jed's emotions died back on the battlefield, and all that remained was a shell of his body. He was simply waiting until his ghost gave up the fight.

Jodi thought he believed he had lost his soul that day when Capt. William Quantrill saw him and drummed him into his ranks. The day after he was attached, he committed his first *mortal sin*—and his second, third, and fourth—he killed eleven men that first day with John Noland. After a while, the numbers blurred. Only he and John knew the truth. The only other person who shared the secret was Capt. Quantrill, but he was shot and killed by Union soldiers only weeks after the war was over. He died in Kentucky, just over the river from his Ohio home.

John had known the captain as well as any man under his command. The man he knew was a fervent fighter and hero of a losing cause. It was hard to imagine him teaching young boys and girls in a school. How did he turn so violent? And what made him believe he could return to an Ohio classroom like nothing ever happened. The Yankee Army made short work of that. There was never any intention to capture William Quantrill. He had already been sentenced to death by the men who hunted him. They sent him to the grave forthwith.

The middle-aged Black man wondered why they wanted him and Jed alive. It made little sense. They would be a hell of a lot harder to capture. Many soldiers would die before they succeeded, without a doubt. It was just a matter of time, like everything else. John felt lucky to have experienced the little freedom he knew. It would have been a shame if he never got to feel what it was like to be a free man, even if he was a wanted outlaw. He was still free until they caught or killed him.

"I finally located a train in Texas," Jodi said. "It's the first of its kind. It only runs eighty miles, but they move money from one town to the other with a giant locomotive. They built it for the ranchers and the railroad companies. I doubt many folks worry about outlaws robbing a train that goes such a short stretch. They are working on more track west, but this is the end of the line."

"In a few years, those forty miles will be four thousand," Jed said. "All trains start from someplace."

The rich aroma of coffee rode on breaths of air. A

woman dressed in black brought a hot pot out to top off their tin cups. The sun blossomed like a red rose making everything appear pink for just a moment before it disappeared. Suddenly, they were plunged into darkness. The only light was the yellow lamplight which spilled from the open cantina door onto the porch. In the middle of nowhere, the sky looked like you could reach out and grab a fistful of stars. Jodi picked out one and made a wish. It was the same wish she had been making for weeks now.

"If the train only stops in two towns, I doubt there be much money on board," Jed said.

"Yeah, but I figured we could use this one to learn what to do and what not to do. We all know how easy it is to make a mistake and get the law on our tails."

The excitement of the challenge was already showing in her eyes. It wasn't long until both Jed and John got the fever, too. After so many years of battle, they found themselves bored. Even though they always looked forward to some quiet time in El Molino, all three were fiddle-footed and hungered for something to spice up their lives. It wasn't for the money. Down in Mexico, they couldn't spend all they'd stolen in ten years.

Jed wondered how long it would be before some bounty hunter got brave enough to show up in their quiet little hideaway. News was hard to keep, and poor people were easy to bribe for information. He felt it was just a matter of time until they caught up to them. It was best they kept on the run and reserved their visits to their hideout for the occasional week of safety and comfort. Jed knew this wouldn't last forever.

More light spilled out of doors and windows as the glow of lit globes of the gasoliers burned overhead.

There were so few people in El Molino they didn't even have a town constable or a jail. How long would this last? Jed knew most good things in his life were doomed for disaster. It had always been that way for him, and he couldn't foresee anything changing.

Of course, Jed Coal knew how Jodi felt for him, and he knew how he felt. He chose to hide his feelings, though. How could he make a promise to settle down when they were all wanted for crimes against the All Mighty, not to mention the banks and casino they robbed. No, he was confident they had little future, and he didn't want to do something to tie Jodi and him at the hip.

Jodi would always have a way out if they came for him and John. She was never there and fought for neither the North nor the South. She really had little to do with all this. That was why Jed was so stubborn with his feelings. He only allowed them to show when she caught him in moments of weakness. She seemed to instinctively know when those moments were, too.

The train ran out of Harrisburg, Texas, just outside of Houston, and all the way to Alleyton. They didn't expect there to be a lot of valuables on the train, but it was the only one in the state, and it was close enough for them to take a look. They decided to go for a ride on the trail to gauge the train's speed, where it slowed down, and if it had to stop anywhere along the way. First, they would enjoy a pleasure cruise. Hopefully, it won't turn out like their pleasure cruise aboard a paddleboat.

CHAPTER 7

SAN ANTONIO SALOON

"Every time we come to San Antonio, we run into the James brothers," John spat. It was clear he was unhappy with their presence. "I figure it's time we change saloons as we've run into that lot twice in the same place. With all the places in town to go, why must they come here?"

"Well, lookee who the cat drug in," Jed said when the brothers looked his way. He pretended to ignore John's displeasure and smiled when he saw them walk into the saloon. Both outlaws walked right over and sat down at their table.

"Where's your sweetheart, Jed?" Jesse asked and grinned.

"She's off shoppin', like most all women who spend time in town," Jed replied, smiling. "What are you two hound dogs doing back in Texas?"

"Running from Kansas law," Frank said. "Ain't nothin' new."

"Don't give me that Quaker in a titty-bar look, Jed,"

the youngest James brother cackled. "You can tell your old pard, Jesse. I won't spill the beans. Is she really your girl? Be honest."

"Only a low-down dog would talk about a woman behind her back. We're southern gentlemen, ain't we?" Jed replied, grinning like a possum.

Jed knew Jesse was a dangerous man, as did most people who knew him well. Jed was a different kind of dangerous, though, and Jesse knew that, too. He'd seen him cold, bloodily walk out into the night behind enemy lines and take soldiers' lives in the dark with no more than a knife, often while they sleep. They didn't even know he was there.

Of course, he knew about his sniper skills, but Jesse had seen Jed draw and shoot, too. He knew he'd be hard-pressed to outdraw him, even though he'd never admit it. It made him respect Jed more than others who rode with Quantrill, including the Younger brothers. But Jesse thought there were leaders, and there were followers. The Youngers were followers, and Jesse was the leader.

He also knew he learned some of his skills from John Noland, the captain's personal scout. He knew he could outdraw and outshoot Noland, but that didn't mean he wasn't as dangerous as any of the three. He taught Jed everything he knew and had also taught Jesse a thing or two when they rode with Bloody Bill Anderson.

Jesse and Frank had formed a gang with Cole Younger and his brothers. Cole was a first-class killer, but some of his brothers were more interested in goofing off and getting drunk than seeking restitution against the Yankee railroads and banks. Jesse, Frank, and Cole were centrally focused.

"Well, if you ain't gonna marry her, I might just ask her myself," Jesse teased Jed.

"She'd marry a polecat before marrying you." Jed laughed. "Jokes aside, nobody's getting married. And you ain't gonna go and flirt with my woman."

"Oh, so now she's your woman," John said, which lightened his mood.

"I don't trust a man with curly hair," Jesse said to John and grinned. "I can't help but imagine small birds laying eggs in there."

You could tell by the look on John's face he didn't like Jesse James very much. The fact John fought with Quantrill, Jesse saw him more as a companion and soldier than a slave. Nonetheless, he never treated him exactly like the other soldiers, though. Jesse was Jesse. Many things he did were hard to explain.

Jodi pushed her way through the bat-wing doors of the saloon. As soon as she saw the James brothers, she frowned, then quickly covered it with a smile that didn't reach her eyes. Her arms were full of packages wrapped in brown paper.

"We robbed the first train in America," Jesse said as his face beamed with pride. "I told ya we could do it. Whatcha got to say about that, ma'am?"

"I would call that braggadocious talk, Mr. James," Jodi replied smartly.

She enjoyed baiting the young outlaw. She lay her purchases on the next table and sat down between Jed and John. She felt safer there. Jesse had a presence that oozed danger, something she had her fill of for a spell.

"Aww, Jesse ain't that bad," Jed said and laughed. He appeared to get along just fine with both the James brothers. "He just takes a little more getting used to than you might have to give." Jed laughed some more. It was like meeting up with old brothers after all they went through together.

The barman came over to take their order. He had ears as big as butterflies, and his smile was so wide his wisdom teeth showed. He immediately caught the attention of the younger James brother.

"What y'all wanna drink? We got white lightning, labeled whiskey, rum, and tequila. We got beer, too, but it might be a tad warm."

"That sounds like a fine start, my good man," Jesse said.

"Exactly what is a fine start, sir?" the barman asked, puzzled.

"Why, just what you said." Jesse laughed. "A bottle of white lightning, a bottle of whiskey, a bottle of rum, and a bottle of tequila. And a beer chaser each—for now. I've got a mighty big thirst."

Frank James just rolled his eyes at his brother, but he didn't bother to complain as he knew it would stir him up more. The rest of them watched as he drank glass after glass of liquor, and it didn't seem to faze him. He had the habit of caressing the leather on his cross-draw pistol. It was something that made folks that didn't know Jesse nervous. When he drank, he acted like always. He sat for a few moments as he talked, then paced back and forth like a tiger in a cage.

Although he found Frank a reasonable man, John still didn't trust Jesse. Jed thought Jesse was a card, and he cracked him up with his jokes and antics the entire evening. Even Jodi eased into things with the notorious outlaw. She willingly joined in with the laughter. Noland maintained a polite smile, but he hardly spoke. Instead, he kept his eyes on Jesse James. He watched both his eyes and his hands. John made a mental note not to return to this hotel and bar again. He didn't actually have anything against the James brothers, but Jesse drew attention like a circus act. He wanted to go unnoticed.

CHAPTER 8

ALLEYTON, TEXAS

WHEN THE THREE OUTLAWS RODE INTO ALLEYTON, TEXAS, the first thing they saw was an enormous train station. It was far too large for such a small town, but the owners built it believing the B.B.B.&C. (Buffalo Bayou, Brazos, and Colorado Railroad) would boost the population and transform Alleyton into a major city. It was named because it was on the Colorado River in Colorado County, Texas. The town boasted a population of a few hundred. The train headed for Harrisburg outside of Houston just eighty miles away.

Jed had started looking at Jodi when she wasn't aware —often at the unlikeliest moments. She liked her olive-skinned beauty, the way her sky-blue eyes sparkled with mischief and the way her long, brunette hair hung below her waist.

Jodi caught him looking and snapped, "What do *you* want?" Her voice sounded much meaner than she intended. She gave him such a look he withered like a flower. Now that he was paying attention to her, she was getting angry. Jed figured he best just give up trying to understand women.

Jodi bought three passages in the first-class carriage and three stables for the horses in the cattle car. When she gave John and Jed their chits, the man she loved was in a broody mood. She didn't know why she spat back at him like she did. It seemed every time he did show interest in her, it was at the wrong time. She was beginning to believe she was almost as ornery and confused as Jed. They were both damaged goods to some extent.

The coach wasn't one of the famous Pulman coaches ridden by the wealthy and affluent. It had plush leather cushions on the benches and bar service for the ride. The train departed with all the fanfare of a cross-country railway. Half the town came to see the train when it came in and out of Alleyton. It was the best thing that ever happened to the tiny community. It promised a future full of growth and wealth, at least for some.

As the engine came to a screeching halt and began to pant, steam poured from every hole in the locomotive. Couplings banged behind the engine as the cars abruptly jarred to a halt. A wood wagon was behind the engine, then came the mail car and the first-class passenger car. After that, there were two second-class carriages for passengers. Next to the end was a platform car full of shiny rails and railroad ties to extend the tacks even farther. Finally, there were some freeloaders on the roof of the caboose. All in all, there were eight carriages beside the locomotive. The conductor hung out the doorway of the engine as he grabbed the railing and looked down the track—then back at the disembarking and boarding passengers.

After thirty minutes, there were two blasts of the

train's whistle, and the large fifty-four-inch wheels slipped at first, then grabbed hold of the track and began to gain momentum. The land was flat, so there were no high grades to climb nor any heavy curves forcing the train to slow down. The engineer ran the train quickly all the way to Harrisburg. It sped down the track at nearly twenty miles per hour.

In no time, they pulled into the station just outside of Houston, Texas. They watched as the cargo carriage opened. It was located between the wood wagon and the first-class passengers. They unloaded several large trunks and a few small ones replaced them. To Jodi, it looked like the large shipments moved from Alleyton to Harrisburg where the big Houston banks were located. She figured it was railway money moving back and forth or payments for large shipments of railroad ties, rails and other construction material.

"It looks like more goods are going out of Harrisburg and into Alleyton than back," Jodi said as she assessed the train. "I wonder how many payrolls are paid out by some big companies depending upon that shipment? Cattlemen and the railroad, I reckon. We're gonna have to do our homework, but I can see this being a start. We may get lucky and get away with a little money too."

"The engineer is all business," John said. "He pulled out of Alleyton on time and didn't stop stoking the fire until they began to slow down for Harrisburg. It took only five and a half hours. That's an eighty-mile ride on horseback."

"Are we gonna stay in town for the night, or are we gonna ride the train back again?" John asked. He was eager to spend more time on the locomotive.

"We don't want to raise suspicions," Jodi whispered.

"We can go back tomorrow. We can check with the post office to see if they do mail service by train, too. Maybe we can get an idea of what goes between the two towns and when."

"We best be looking for a hotel then," John said, but his eyes stared at the soot and smoke-spewing contraption. This was the first time he'd ridden on a train. He never imagined he would have the opportunity. Life never stopped surprising the ex-slave.

Later that evening, John swigged his beer as John sipped at a whiskey and casually cocked his head. Jodi was scratching on a yellow notepad with a two-bit pencil in her fist. The draft through the open window teased the candle's flame. As Jodi read, yellow light flickered on her face as her fingers scribbled sentences. This time when Jed watched, she didn't notice. She was wholly absorbed in the details of their train ride.

"What if the train don't have any money on it?" John asked.

"There could be payrolls on board if we could figure when their hands got paid." Jodi said. "There could be both cattle and railroad money onboard. We'd have to steal the money while it's still on the train, or the railroad company won't compensate them for their loss. We gotta do this right and not steal from innocent folks. I believe the railroads be as wicked as any of the banks."

Jodi even made friends with the engineer. When she saw him eating at the diner, she dropped her purse beside his chair. He fell all over himself to help the pretty lady. Of course, he bragged about his position on the railway.

"Without me, the train won't move an inch," he bragged. "It's a tricky thing to engineer a powerful locomotive. Today we took just over five hours to get here, but I could do it in four if I opened her up. She'll do the better part of thirty miles an hour flat out—maybe a tad more. I'll swear to that."

"Ever since I was a little girl, I dreamed of riding up there in the engineer's cabin," Jodi said as her eyes twinkled at the rough old cob. "My ma said my granddaddy was a railroad man, but he died before I was born." When Jodi's eyes teared up at the mention of her dear, departed grandfather, the engineer became butter in her hands.

"If you plan to return to Alleyton, you just show up by the engine, and I'll show ya around. I might even let you pull the whistle's cable."

"You would?" Jodi asked with wide eyes of innocence. She was one hell of an actor.

Or was she? With Jodi, you just never knew. She may have taken a sudden fancy to trains for all John and Jed knew. She was chock-full of surprises with a wagonload of energy. Sometimes she wore the two men out. Neither man had ever seen such a sponge for information.

When they climbed aboard the train to return to Alleyton the next day, Jodi was standing by the powerful locomotive with her cowgirl duds on, ready to learn all she could about running a twenty-two-ton train. She immediately scrambled up to the engine room beside the engineer. The man was as pleased as punch to have a pretty Texas gal accompany him and the fireman for the trip back. So, she could learn all she could, Jodi was a nightmare of questions. Their men's hearts melted when she batted her eyelashes and they held nothing back.

"Come on, Roger," she said to the engineer. "Let's see how fast she'll really go."

Engineer Roger Loring and Fireman Rodney Randolph fell all over themselves to show which one knew the most. Of course, Roger was the engineer, so he was the boss, but the fireman worked right beside him. There was nothing the two were unwilling to share.

Of course, the fireman had the backbreaking job of keeping the boiler fire full of wood or coal. Jodi even pitched in and threw a few dozen logs into the fire. By the time they arrived at their destination, Jodi knew pretty much how to operate a train all on her own. She spent the entire trip in the engine room.

She seemed like a little girl when she skipped down the station platform. Of course, the twenty-six-year-old woman could pass for a sixteen-year-old. Jed's heart couldn't help but skip a beat as he saw how she smiled, and her eyes twinkled as she danced their way.

John let out a laugh. Lately, he laughed at nearly everything. Being free seemed to do him a world of good, even though they were all wanted by the law. At least he could do what he wanted to do for a change and not follow the orders of some officer or plantation owner.

CHAPTER 9

SERGEANT ROOSTER BEASTLY

THE CAPTAIN AT FORT MACINTOSH STROLLED UP AND down the barracks porch as his fury got the best of him. The Quantrill outlaws escaped his grasp at Port Lavaca, and now he heard someone saw them near Laredo. By now, he believed they could be already down in Mexico. Captain Rayland Gash was not a patient man, and when he got on someone's trail, he wouldn't give up until he ran them to ground. He never quit, and the Rio Grande would not stop him from capturing these rascals.

They not only murdered a ship's captain in his jurisdiction, but a second unidentified man was killed by somebody still unknown. He suspected Coal and Noland had something to do with that death, too. He planned to get to the bottom of the case sooner rather than later. He had never figured out what happened there aboard the Texas Belle. The other man had no identification or even a newspaper clipping, but he had all the markings of a Kansas Marauder. They believed him to be a bushwhacker as most Jayhawkers rode with red leggings.

If the south was to heal, such men had to be run down, shot and buried. Captain Gash felt until these treasonous rebels were executed, there would be no chance for peace. Even with the war over, violence still ran rampant on the border with Kansas and Missouri.

He was a decorated officer from the Civil War and felt a deep hatred for all Southerners. He even disliked the Texans, who didn't get properly involved one way or another in the Civil War. Sure, they were on the side of the Confederacy, but few fought, and more spent their time in Texas wreaking mayhem while the war raged.

The major hailed from the iconic city of Boston and found no others to be its equal when it came to the US Constitution and the American cause. His fever often affected his judgment. He turned a blind eye to the atrocities carried out by the men of the Union army and wreaked the wrath on those Southerners that committed the same or lesser crimes. Gash believed the victors got the spoils. It was just too bad for the losers.

They sent the captain's best man, Sergeant Rooster Beastly, to the northern plains to assist the US Calvary in tracking and defeating the last of the Sioux. He was a renowned Indian fighter and a decorated scout throughout the Civil War. Beastly was a hardened warrior, a mercenary of sorts, for lack of a better term.

If he had an enemy to track, he would run them down no matter how he had to do it. If he got paid for his tasks, that is. He did nothing for family or country—not anymore. For Beastly, patriotism was a thing of the past. He only worked for hard currency or silver coins. There were no exceptions. He felt he'd given everything to his country, and now it was time for him to get something back.

Captain Gash chose to ignore this, considering his record in hunting down wanted men. While Beastly was about money, the captain was more interested in power. With power came money like the scout never imagined. The captain's plan was long term. He had his sights set on Washington as a military adviser. If he was to capture the last of Quantrill's Raiders, he would gain notice. That would be the coup de grâce. He knew other men had tired in their flight south, but he was no ordinary officer. He had skills the others didn't. He was a hard-core warrior and didn't give a damn what he had to do to get what he wanted.

Rooster had ridden with the captain off and on for the last fifteen years. He had no real ties to either the North or the South; he simply worked for the highest bidder. He chose wisely and when he joined the northern, industrialized states to defend during the war, although his origins were always a subject of question. Some said he was from the South; others said he was a Yankee. His light skin and hazel eyes made him unmistakably a White man. Other than that, he never claimed to be from the same place twice. It was a mystery held dear and enjoyed.

It was also good to keep your enemies from knowing your origins. A clever hunter will use friends and family to get to the outlaws they want. Of course, innocent people often got trampled and plowed over along the way. That was the way of all wars.

Rooster wore the buckskins of the northern tribes. He kept his hat slapped up in the front like men of the Seventh Cavalry. He also wore regulation boots and an officer's sword, even though he wasn't officially in the Army any longer. He was a mercenary with little discipline, but he always got his man. He wagered his reputation on it.

Rooster's long brown hair hung well below his shoulders. He had two scalps sewn onto one of the sleeves of his buckskins. He wore a bear claw necklace and a piece of pigging string around his wrist with a dried rattler's tail hanging from it. He wore a necklace under his buckskin shirt with what looked like dried slices of potatoes. They were the ears of his enemies. He seemed half hostile and half mountain man and meaner than a snake.

Rooster rode a spotted mustang with as many scars as Rooster. He was a tall, thin man who oozed danger at first glance. He was as fast as a viper and was known to strike first and without warning. He wore a brace of pistols with the handles forward and two revolvers in shoulder holsters. He had a small six-shooter hidden in a boot and a knife in the other.

A long scar, left from a Pawnee tomahawk, ran from his left eyebrow to his right cheek. He was missing two fingers on his left hand. He lost his pinky and ring finger to angry Comanche, who he killed soon after. He bore the scars of his wars with pride. He stood before gunfire throughout the Civil War like he was invincible. He neither flinched nor shied from bullets.

When he attacked a man with a smile and guns blazing, most men's legs weakened, and their aim went astray. Seeing the hunger for death in his eyes left many men in shock and provided him with just enough time to shoot and kill.

Even Captain Gash overlooked some of Beasley's murderous ways. All that mattered was for the job to get done, and Rooster did so as much viciousness as anyone had seen. For the Indian fighter, it mattered little who his target was. He was only interested in getting paid; killing was his occupation.

All Captain Gash needed was the location on the fleeing marauders. He had notified Indian scouts along the border, from Laredo to Eagles Pass, to watch for the fugitives. Now, all he could do was wait until someone gave them up. He knew his wait wouldn't be long.

TWO THIN INDIANS waited on the edge of the treelined outside Eagles Pass. One was tall with his hair in two braids. The other had a similar build, but he wore feathers in dozens of small trances that sprouted from his head like a small octopus. Both men patiently waited and watched who came and went from the Rick Pawless Trading Post.

A stagecoach pulled up, and several women spilled out onto the street. The stagecoach ride had been more discomfort than most of them ever imagined. The Tonkawa Indians waited for them to unload the coach. Then, they crossed the street and wandered into the trading post. The Pawless Post was one of the few places local Indians came to trade. Even though the fort was only a couple of miles away, Indians, trappers, and pioneers frequented the trading post ever since the Indians could remember.

Seth Kinman was one of the first frontiersmen to stay at the Rick's when he crossed the southern United States on foot. He crossed America, from coast to coast, seven times in all, and he walked every foot of the way.

The room was full of women in bad-smelling dresses and men with sweat stains on their backs and under their arms. Most wore pistols strapped to their waists.

Rick and Mini stood behind the bar. It was a series of wooden barrels with thick timber planks across the top.

"Well, look who the cat done drug in," Rick said with a smile. He was a massive man with hands as big as hams. His size and past reputation made him a man with whom few frolicked. Rick Pawless only knew how to play one way, and most often it was deadly.

"We came around to see a friend," Potak said as he eyed the ladies of the night and wrinkled his nose. The men smelled like polecats, and the women smelled like whores. "I don't see any of your friends around here lately."

"We are lookin' for a Lipan Apache by the name of Chatto. He lives near a little Mexican village in the desert."

"I know who ya mean, but he's done come and gone," Rick said. "Was he supposed to meet up with y'all? I saw him walk off with a captain from the fort and some fella that looked like an Indian fighter from the northern plains. I'd venture to say he be a dangerous one, that fella."

Potak shook his head and appeared disgusted. When Indians were willing to sell gossip to the Army rather than friends something was amiss. The problem with Chatto was he was foolish and dumb. He would give the Blue Coats anything they wanted to know for a few dollars. He would lead them to his tribe's village south of the border if he weren't careful. Then the money they paid him for gossip would be for nothing because he deceived his people.

Tuc and Potak decided to hang around the outside of Fort Duncan so they could keep an eye on the activities. Maybe they would even see Chatto if the soldiers hadn't locked him up. Sometimes the soldiers wanted to guarantee an informant's information was correct. So, they kidnapped them until they were assured a trap was not part of the plan. It was a complicated business buying and selling gossip. Indians had to be cautious and clever. Unfortunately, Chatto was neither.

They waited all day in the shadows provided by the shacks that dotted the land all around the fort. A variety of inhabitants lived just outside the log walls. Some were immigrants who ran into Comanche or Apache and stayed where they could take cover in case of attack. There were even a few Indians who lived in teepees and did odd chores for a few pennies. Most of the people who lived outside the fort lived in poverty.

The occupants of the fort were another thing, though. Most of the officers had their families living in nice little houses inside the safety of the walls. The gate was open during the day, although guards were on turrets on both sides. These men were the first defenders against hostile attacks. An orderly came to Captain Gash's office and said the scout with the Indian gossip on Quantrill's men were outside.

"Send him to me immediately," Captain Gash snapped.

The soldier ran off, and in less than five minutes, the poor Lipan Apache was standing before a Blue Coat chief. By chance, Beastly entered at the same time and the Indian got nervous. His eyes gravitated to the black scalps on his buckskins.

"This is Chatto," the private who brought him in said. "Will that be all, sir?"

"Leave us alone for a minute, private. Close the door behind you. We need to have a conversation with this Apache," Gash advised.

"I am Lipan Apache. We are not enemies."

"You are to me, you little thief," Rooster growled. "Spit it out now! Tell us all you know suffer the consequences."

Chatto appeared ready to sing his death song. He hadn't counted on there being an Indian killer at the negotiations. Usually, selling gossip was a simple matter. He knew the two Tonkawa cousins made a good living peddling information. But he saw he had made a mistake. He suddenly realized the Blue Coats might ride into El Molino and kill the villagers along with the gringos. He hoped to make a single silver eagle. Now he saw he would be lucky if he escaped with his life.

The problem with Chatto was he was dumber than a dog's foot. He inadvertently walked into the devil's castle and straight into the dragon's jaws. He couldn't take his eyes off Rooster. He could see the man wanted to kill him.

"Before you two go at it, we might want to calm down a bit," Capt. Gash said. "One Apache is not the issue here. This is far more important than a few starving hostiles. Look at the man. He's skin and bones."

Finally, he turned to Chatto and asked, "I know this information is not free, so how much do you want? Before you answer, I want to remind you if you lie to me in any detail, I will hunt you down and kill you, your wife, your children, your mother and your father. Do you understand?"

"My English is good. I visit Eagles Pass often. My information is true. My price is one silver dollar, a single eagle."

Captain Gash didn't even complain. He pulled a ring of keys out of the top drawer, turned to a strongbox, and opened the door. He pulled a shiny silver dollar out and locked it tight again. He placed it in his palm and held it out to Chatto. The Indian tried to snatch the coin from his hand, but the captain was quick. He laughed as he taunted the Apache.

"Now give me the location of the men from Missouri, the rifleman and the Black man. Where are they, and how far away is it from here?" he demanded.

"They are in a small village called El Molin," Chatto replied. He realized he might be signing a death warrant for all the people who lived there for a silver coin. He pushed the thought from his mind and told himself he was overthinking everything. Selling gossip was simple if you allowed it to be.

"Take him out back and shoot him, Rooster," Captain Gash said like he was talking about the weather. "Have my private outside the door arrange for a detail to plant him wherever they bury the hostiles they kill these days."

"And the silver eagle?" Rooster asked.

"Call it a bonus on top up your wages." Captain Gash chuckled. "I think we're going to get to go to a party. And it's just the kind of party I like."

Beastly took the liberty of changing the captain's orders slightly. It was just enough to give that extra touch Rooster liked to add to his work, but not so much as to get a reprimand. He pushed his hand into his britches and fingered the silver coin.

Chatto was hung from the tree, his neck broken and

his hands and arms hanging limply. Burns covered his face, apparently made by the tip of a cigar. He had a broken leg, and the jagged end of a white bone stuck out of his britches.

They left him to swing in the breeze. A note was tacked to his shirt. It read. *"REDSKINS BEWARE! ROOSTER IS IN TOWN!"*

CHAPTER 10

RUN AWAY TRAIN

THE THREE STAYED IN A LOW-PROFILE HOTEL IN ALLEYTON the following week. It was called *The Bavarian House Hotel & Fine Dining*. The trio claimed they were looking for some land to purchase for a group of cattlemen. Jodi went as far as to visit the two biggest banks in town to see what they had repossessed from poor ranchers who fell on hard times

This gave her insight into which banks held the most money. The town was busy. New buildings were springing up as merchants looked to the future when the railroad would go farther north, south, east, and west. Then this little town would become a city. At least, that was what the general business owners believed.

Buckboard wagons were slanted up to the businesses along the street as women in white bonnets strolled the boardwalk. Children hid under the shadows of the walkway, with their chins propped up in the palms of their hands watching wagons go by with eyes spread wide. Several horses drank water from troughs at hitching rails. Everything in town appeared to be normal. The sun was a few hours from the horizon, and the heat began to wane.

This was the end of the line for the railroad, but they already were working on extending the tracks farther west toward San Antonio. This was where Jodi discovered they shipped the largest payrolls at the end of every month. It was the money to pay the labor for laying railroad ties and tracks that snaked across the countryside like some endless man-made scar.

A robbery would hurt the railroad and concern the bankers and wealthy ranchers. The ones that were already open also shipped their money on the same train, but it appeared on random days for the most part.

Jed decided it would pay to stake the banks out. He wanted to observe when money moved from the bank's vaults to the train. They found that most banks had little rhyme or reason when they sent their irregular shipments. Maybe when they reached a certain amount, the main branch would want to hold the capital. They were clustered in the town square, a common practice of banks. Jed and John kept watch from an hour before they opened to an hour after the last employee left. In each case, the bank director was last to leave and close up shop. They were also the first to arrive. They narrowed their targets down to two banks, which stood catty-corner.

Since there was no way to determine when the banks made the shipments, they had to devise an alternative plan. In small towns like these, most folks never even considered the possibility of a bank or train getting robbed.

The three outlaws sat around a table in the saloon next to the quaint hotel. A bottle of whiskey sat in the middle with three empty glasses. Jed and John spent several days riding the tracks on horseback. Between the two towns, they saw no place where the train would slow down enough for them to jump on board from a running horse. It was too dangerous for both man and animal.

"There's no way we can catch the train on horseback," John said. "If the train ain't running flat out, we might ride that fast, but it'd be another matter trying to climb aboard a rocking locomotive from a running horse. The only way I can see it happening is if we're on the train. Then we have the problem of stopping it wherever we stash the horses so we can escape. We can have fresh horses and a change of clothing waiting a few hours away. We can hide the money by the freshwater spring a day north of El Molino."

"First, we have to get into the locked car," Jodi said. "Then we've got to see what's worth taking and what's not. If we do it right, we won't even have to hurry. The folks on board won't know a thing until the train stops halfway to Harrisburg."

"The question is, how are we gonna stop the loco-motive once we've got the money?" Jed asked. "The getting on is easy enough. We can buy tickets and board the train like any other passengers. But if we wait until we get to Columbus, we'll have the sheriff waiting for us."

"That's the easiest part," Jodi said. "I have an idea of how to make this work and give us at least a day or two head start on the posse. I reckon they'll have their hands full for a spell before they speak to anyone who witnessed what happened."

"Whatcha got in mind?" Jed asked.

"If I can talk my way back in with the engineer and get the drop on them, we can steal the train."

"Now you're talking nonsense," John said. "That's ridiculous. What you'll do is get us all killed. Trains be dangerous, and them engineers are skilled professionals."

"Anyone with half a brain can pull a few levers and watch some pressure gauges. If we do it as I say, nobody will get hurt, and we're going to hold up the train for a good spell. It will take them a while to figure out what happened. We steal from the railroads and rich Yankee bankers, and we don't hurt any poor folks. I had my ranch taken from me by a bank, and I wouldn't mind a little payback."

"Both bankers in town are bachelors. So, they won't have anybody waiting for them at home," Jed said as he mused another idea. "Maybe John and I can guarantee some profits for our effort, and we can learn about robbing trains while getting paid for it. We already know how to rob banks."

Both Jed and John exchanged glances, but they'd see Jodi come up with some pretty bodacious ideas before, and they all worked out fine. At least when John and Jed had heeded her instruction. Finally, they figured there was little left to lose.

"What time does the train pull out to return to Harrisburg?" Jed asked.

"It pulls out at six sharp," Jodi replied. "The ride was just over five hours long."

The cowgirl from Waco, Texas, stared into her glass of tequila and swirled the yellow liquid. Jodi appeared to be looking into a magic crystal to see their future. Jed and John tossed their drinks back and were ready to leave.

"I think this is gonna work out in our favor," Jed said. "Come on, John. We got some work to do."

THE BACHELORS who managed the two largest banks in town came from larger banks in the state's capital. Those financial giants were part of larger ones back East. It took lots of Yankee money to build the railroad. Everybody expected Alleyton to be a thriving hub with the railway extension. Harrisburg was already growing and prosperous. It boasted a population of thousands. Both men seemed to spend most of their week at their respective offices. Both departed at least an hour after their banks closed and arrived at least an hour before they opened. Both men appeared to be workaholics.

When they opened an hour early, there were no employees present. The Stanford Savings and Trust manager was always the first to arrive, followed by the banker from the building across the square. Jed and John intended to rob both banks in less than an hour and get to the train before it departed.

The two had come up with the plan on their own. Neither one saw sense in robbing a train that might not have anything of value, even if Jodi thought it was a learning experience. If they robbed the banks first, they would already have their money. Then they would steal the train to get away.

When they sat around the table the night before, it seemed clear and straightforward as they finished off a bottle of tequila.

When Jed knocked on the bank's glass door the next morning, it seemed to be a hard nut to crack without notifying the whole town. The manager sat at his desk with several stacks of money. He was wrapping each one and logging the quantity on a piece of paper. The last thing he expected was an outlaw to be standing at his door in plain sight with a pistol pointing his way. From where he sat, the black barrel appeared huge. John stood with his back to Jed and the door, so nobody on the street could see his gun.

As Jed's barrel followed the manager to the door, he hoped he didn't die from a heart attack before he got it open. His blood pressure was so high several blood vessels throbbed at his temples and another at his neck.

"Hold on there, pard," Jed said as he grabbed the man's arm to steady him. "Don't fall. I apologize, but we're in a mighty big hurry, so the sooner you show us the money, the sooner we'll leave, and you won't have this gun pointing at ya anymore."

All he had to do was look over at the safe. The door stood three inches open. The name on the outside said Mossler Safe Co. Hamilton, Ohio. John raked the money the manager was counting on his desk into a bag as Jed went for the safe.

"It ain't a fortune, but it was worth the time," Jed said. Then he turned to the manager. "Are you sure there's no more money here?" Then he turned the gun on the banker and pulled back the hammer.

"The rest is on the train headed for Columbus," the manager replied. He averted his eyes from both men. He was scared to death and acted like he didn't want to have to identify them later.

"I'm sorry," he said as tears ran down his cheeks.

Jed almost felt sorry for him until he remembered it was bankers who took Jodi's ranch and the homes and farms of many others, especially after the war. Banks, backed with Yankee money, bought up cheap land from bankrupted businesses and plantations.

John quickly tied the manager to his chair and walked to the door. It was then he noticed the other manager was searching for the key to unlock the door to the bank across the way. He and John had to move fast.

"Finish this up, and I'll catch that Yankee before anybody else shows up," John said as he turned to run. "I want to catch him before he finds the key and locks himself in."

John ran for the other boardwalk with his pistol in his hand. A pistol-packing Black man running down the middle of the street in broad daylight was cause for alarm in the South, especially just after the war. Women dropped what they had in their hands and ran for their lives. Others fainted, while men took cover.

"Don't turn around, mister," John said. "Now open that door slow, like cold molasses. If you're careful, I might not shoot ya."

When they went inside, the safe was locked tight as a drum, and the Wells Fargo Bank manager was not the coward they found at the Stanford Point Savings and Loan. John pushed him to the safe, but he stood there and crossed his arms defiantly.

"So, you want to be difficult, do ya?" John asked as cool as ice. "I have no problem with that."

Then John pulled the trigger. A hole appeared in the banker's foot. At first, he stared at the gaping wound and torn leather and watched as blood quickly pooled under his shoe. Then the pain hit, and he howled like a banshee. John pointed his revolver to his temple and whispered in a voice that sounded very much like death.

"A White man just like you owned me for the better part of my life," John whispered, his voice low and dangerous. "It wouldn't bother me a bit to shoot you dead unless you open that safe."

"My foot!" he gasped.

"You'll have a hole somewhere else if you don't hurry, and this time it won't be in your foot. So, stop the sass," John spat. "I'm plumb out of patience."

Suddenly, Jed rapped on the bank window with his knuckles. A dozen people saw John run for the banker with a pistol, and half the town heard the shot. Just down the street, two blasts sounded from the steam whistle on the locomotive. That was the single for all to board as it was preparing to depart.

When John came out with a canvas satchel full of money, Jed said, "I thought we would do this nice and quiet. Now, half the town knows we done robbed the banks."

"Yeah, but they don't know we're stealing the train too," John said, grinning. "Ain't it grand being free?"

They both turned for the train. Fear caught up with their legs as they raced for the caboose. They ran down the railroad ties as they closed in on the ladder to the last red wagon. Jed reached for the steel rung and missed, nearly falling. As they ran harder, they exchanged knowing glances. Again, they hadn't followed the plan, and now the train was getting away from them. If they didn't make it on the caboose, the townsfolk would be right behind them. They would lynch them before the sun set.

Fear-produced adrenaline gave them the final energy boost they needed to make one last stab for the railing. Holding tight, the departing train pulled them off their feet. In seconds they were safely standing on the back platform of the caboose. They knew they still had to make it to the engine, but both of them were out of breath and had stitches on their sides. After gasping for a couple of minutes, they climbed up the ladder to the roof of the now roaring locomotive. They ran across the length of the caboose. They came to the flatbed carriage with the railroad supplies and five workers.

Jed and John pointed their pistols at the men relaxing on the car. Their eyes spread wide when they saw a White man and a Black man pointing revolvers at them.

"Adios, boys," Jed said as he flicked the barrel of his pistol, indicating they vacate the flatbed. "You can jump or you can get shot and pushed off. Of course, then you'll be dead. So, what's it gonna be? Jump now or take your last breath."

All five men stood and stepped to the edge of the carriage. The engine was picking up speed.

"It's now or never, lads," Jed said as he gave the first one a push with the sole of his boot. The other four jumped right after.

They still had to get through the two second-class passenger cars and the first-class carriage. The outlaws stood on either side of the door that led into the last passenger coach. Jed stole a glance, and it mainly appeared empty.

"Let's act like we're just a couple of passengers," Jed whispered. "They have no reason to doubt us."

John nodded, slipped his gun back into his holster, and carried the satchel of money in front of him. He eyed each passenger as they passed. Most were busy reading or talking. They pushed their way through the door at the end of the carriage, finding themselves on the platform between cars.

"Two more to go," Jed said as he peeked through the glass window.

He saw four Yankee soldiers horse-playing at the other end of the car. They knew there was no way they could pass without being noticed and hoped the men hadn't seen their likeness on wanted posters.

"How do we do it?" John asked, his brow furrowed with concern.

"Listen to this," Jed said as he whispered.

His friend's idea got a doubtful look, but he had faith in the sniper's judgment. Trust had allowed them to save each other's life on several occasions.

When a big Black man pushed his way into the second passenger wagon with a fistful of Jed's shirt collar and a pistol to his head, he spat and cussed up a storm. All four Blue Coats turned. So did everyone in the carriage. They stopped what they were doing and looked on in shock. A few jaws dropped because it wasn't every day you saw a Black man manhandling a White man. The Yankee soldiers were half-drunk from the looks of things, and they loved it. John immediately had all their attention.

"I caught me one," John called out to the soldiers. "Come on, boys. Help me throw him off the train. They say he was a Missouri bushwhacker."

By this time, the two outlaws were standing over the soldiers who had yet to get to their feet. Pistols cracked against four skulls, leaving the recipients out cold and worthless for the next hour or two. They would have some bad headaches when they came around, but they'd still be alive. Blood ran down their motionless faces.

Next, they burst through the doors to the first-class carriage. As they suspected, they weren't going to have any trouble with the rich folks. All their faces immediately turned ashen and pale.

They walked through the car unhindered. John turned back, looked at Jed and asked, "What if we rob the rich folks, too?"

"What?" Jed asked, believing maybe he had misheard. He stared at John. When he didn't reply, he knew he was serious. "All right, why not? Most of 'em probably won't notice the loss."

Jed dropped the bag to the floor, pulled his other pistol, and called out, "This is a train robbery. My associate here, Mr. Black, will be passing around a bag. I want you to put your money in it. It won't hurt so much if you be good and consider this as a special tax to benefit poor folks."

Several men put their fancy gold or silver watches in the bag. John considered the items things White men owed him for a long time.

When a woman began to pull off her wedding band, Jed said, "No wedding rings from men or women. We're folks from the South and have a certain respect for women. Excuse us for the interruption. We appreciate the donation. It'll go to a good cause, I promise."

"Are you ready, Mr. White?" John chuckled.

Jed nodded and they drug the heavier sack and satchel behind them. They stood before the mail and special baggage car. They knew better than to try to force their way in now. The money wagon and the man inside were already in Jodi's plan. They scrambled up the ladder on the one end, ran across the top of the carriage, and down the ladder on the other end. They found themselves behind the wood wagon. It was the carriage sandwiched between them and Jodi in the cab of the locomotive.

There was a narrow walkway along the side with a thin rail to grab hold of, but they didn't dare try it with the heavy bags full of money and jewelry. With no other obvious choice, they climbed the pile of firewood from the engine's boiler. Black soot and smoke covered their faces from the roaring engine as they climbed the mountain of logs.

They saw how fast the trees and ground passed them when they looked down. The wind hammered against their faces. The long wide trail of black smoke coming out of the stack was thick and dark. Blasts of white steam blew holes in the black soot. The engineer and the fireman were both bound and gagged in the corner.

"It feels like she's running her flat out," Jed yelled over the roaring engine. "She's a character, that woman. Ya gotta love her."

Jed didn't even notice he said it, but John heard. He wondered if John knew what he had said? He knew he was innocent when it came to women. In one way, he was an old man who had seen and done far too much for the human mind to take. On the other hand, a happy young man in there occasionally revealed himself.

Maybe there was a chance for Jed to forget his demons.

CHAPTER 11

MAYHEM

JODI WALKED TOWARD THE ENGINE IN A NEW WHITE DRESS at a quarter to six. She carried saddlebags in her right hand as her hips swayed. The snow-white dress made her suntan glisten. The front revealed enticing cleavage. Every man she passed tipped their hat and greeted her. Today in the sunshine, her sky-blue eyes hypnotized every male she gazed upon. She was putting on a show. The steam hissed under the wheels of the Baldwin loco-motive, lifting Jodi Goodnight's dress as she struggled to keep it from flying over her head. She quickly looked around but didn't see Jed or John. Men on the platform averted their eyes like they hadn't noticed.

Miss Goodnight had no problem talking the engineer and the fireman into letting her ride with them again. The engineer even wore his best cap and bib overalls and loaned his extra conductor's cap to Jodi. As they prepared to leave Alleyton and head back to Harrisburg, Jodi carefully watched everything they did to run the massive engine. She found it easier than one would expect. The woman had a knack for picking up things, and this gigantic twenty-two-ton monster was no exception. She figured if a man could do it, so could she.

She grew up on a ranch with lots of men who were as rough as corn cobs. Her father never had the son he wanted. So Jodi was thrown into the task of running a ranch. She quickly found she had more skills than many men on the spread. She was a good listener and watched every detail of each chore she learned. For her, running a train as big as a house was a challenge for which she felt entirely prepared.

"What's in the saddlebags, ma'am?" the fireman asked. Middle-aged and polite, the two men had difficulty keeping their eyes off Jodi's shapely figure.

"You don't expect me to help you run this train in my Sunday dress, do ya?" the Texas beauty said. "You two be gentlemen and turn your eyes while I change into my denim britches and a flannel shirt. Promise you won't peek?"

She was out of her dress and pulling on her pants and shirt right before she wrapped her gun belt around her waist and buckled it up. She pulled her six-shooter, spun the chamber, and slipped it back in her holster.

Jodi's fingers curled and uncurled beside the walnut handle of his revolver as she stood behind the fireman who was stoking the boiler full to build steam. The engineer was busy looking up and down the tracks to make sure all was clear for his departure. When they turned, they looked down the dark barrel of a revolver.

"Reach for the sky, boys." Jodi smiled. "If you two gentlemen do like I say, you'll come out of this smelling like roses. And if you don't, I think you can both imagine what y'all is gonna smell like."

You could see the shock in the wood chucker's eyes,

but the engineer genially appeared to have his feelings hurt. It was clear he had a crush on Jodi, and her turning out to be an outlaw shattered his heart.

Jodi smiled and tapped his face with her hand, and said, "I hope I ain't hurt your feelings after you've been so nice, but I'm afraid I'm going to steal your train."

A look of disbelief crossed both men's faces. Clearly, they didn't quite understand what the pretty but dangerous woman was saying.

There were only six cars, including the caboose. Three passenger cars and one flatbed wagon full of railroad equipment, track, and ties. Barrels of steel spikes accompanied the equipment. Several railroad workers rode in the open wagons cooling off on a blistering hot day. The mail car was right behind the woodbin and at the end of it, all was a red caboose.

Between the engine and the first-class passenger car came the mail wagon. That would be where they kept the money. Jodi grabbed the cord and pulled the whistle twice to warn Jed and John it was time to leave. She had no idea where her partners were. They had promised to keep to the plan, so she had to take them at their word. She got ready to leave without them.

DEAD BUGS, varmints, and tumbleweed covered the cowcatcher. Soot and smoke rolled black out of the tea-kettle smokestack as white steam spewed out of pipes and nozzles. The train roared, leaving an ugly black stain on the sky as the engine panted faster with each breath of the boiler. The churning wheels began to grip, and the locomotive lurched forward, gaining momentum as it began to roar down the track.

Jodi had yet to notice Jed and John's presence as she stoked the boiler. Both men had a bag of money in one hand and a pistol in the other when they climbed out of the wood wagon. When they looked down, they saw Jodi from the back—and she was running the train. She craned her head and peered back with a crazed look in her eyes. She looked obsessed. Then a grin spread from cheek to cheek, flashing white teeth and a look of joy. She was having the time of her life. She noticed the bags of money in their hands. For a second, they saw anger burst across her features. The men hadn't followed the plan—again.

The roar of the engine running at full speed was mind-boggling. They could hardly think. Jodi pointed to the pile of wood and the boiler door. Jed and John got to work building up more steam to push the locomotive past thirty miles per hour. The speedometer continued to climb along with the pressure gauge on the boiler. They wanted to make it to the halfway point as soon as possible.

Finally, Jodi told the boys to stop stoking the fire and she began to release steam from the boiler. The train started to slow. The drive cylinders brakes and the 54-inch steel wheels screeched against the rails as the iron beast slowed to a halt. The massive weight continued from the inertia as sparks flew from the wheels turning the orange with heat.

They finally stopped with sequential jolts as each car banged into the next carriage's couplings. Surprised by the stoppage in the middle of nowhere, curious passengers looked out the windows. A couple of men wandered down the steps, unaware the train was being robbed. Or better said, the train had been stolen, lock, stock, and smoking barrel of black soot and smoke.

Jed and John grabbed the horses and rode up and down the passenger cars ordering the occupants to step down and head for the tree line.

"All right, folks," Jed called out as he swung back into the passenger car. "Everybody out—and I mean now!"

A few protested, but that was cut short with a look into Jed's eyes and the barrel of his Colt Walker revolver.

Jodi cut the engineer and fireman loose. The fireman was scared when he saw Jed and John. Both men looked dangerous. The engineer was still heartbroken Jodi had taken advantage of him.

"I'm so sorry, honeybunch," she said. "You were such a sweet man to teach me how to run a train. I'll never forget your kindness."

She kissed his cheek. The big man blushed and almost smiled. Jed led both shaken men down the ladders. All the passengers disembarked, too. Finally, all that could be heard was the panting of the steam engine.

"Now, for those of you who know how to walk, all you have to do is follow these tracks for a few hours, depending on how slow or fast you go. It's forty miles either way," Jed said. "If you follow the rails, you can't get lost. I'm afraid we have other plans for the train."

There were immediate protests from the wealthy people who had no intention of walking God only knew how many hours to Harrisburg. Some of the women were in high-heeled shoes. It could take them days.

"Calm down, all of ya," John said. "As soon as this here train arrives with nobody on it, I'm sure they'll come back and pick you all up."

"Let's get that mail car open," Jed said. "Times-a-wasting."

John and Jed wheeled their horses around and hurried back to the sliding door on the mail car and banged on it with their fists.

"I know you're in there," Jed yelled. "We've already disembarked all the passengers because we plan to run the train into the Harrisburg station and blow it up. I just thought I'd give you a chance to save yourself."

A voice came from inside. "How do I know you're telling the truth?"

"Suit yourself, partner," Jed said. "I already robbed your rich passengers, so we can take or leave whatever you got in there. It's up to you. You got five seconds, or the train pulls out."

In seconds, they heard the door unlatch. Then it slid open. The man at the door looked down at four dark pistol barrels. Jed and John had him covered if he came out shooting.

He threw his hands into the air, screamed, and pleaded, "Don't shoot me, please!" He tumbled out of the wagon and rolled on the ground. He quickly got to his feet and ran for the tree line with the other passengers.

"Let's see what we got," Jed said to John.

John nudged his horse level with the carriage floor and climbed aboard. When he opened the sacks, he found the money from the bank back in Alleyton. His smile flashed two rows of white teeth. They had hit the jackpot!

Now, they had to get away.

Jed nodded to Jodi, who was still up in the engine room. John climbed aboard beside her and began to stoke the boiler as Jodi pulled the cord several times, making the whistle scream and announce the train's renewed departure. Suddenly the engine banged into motion with a jolt, making the couplings clank. The wheel eccentrics dropped, and the fifty-four-inch drive wheels began to churn and spin again, making sparks fly from the steel rails.

The couplings banged as the wheels gripped, one after the other, and the empty carriages began to move forward and sway, headed for Harrisburg. Jodi Goodnight was standing on the boarding step with one hand grasping the cab rail as he leaned out to see what was ahead. She still wore the engineer's cap they gave her.

They ran hard for three hours running the engine flat out. About twenty minutes outside of Columbus, Jed came running up alongside the train with fresh horses. Jodi slowed the locomotive down to about fifteen miles per hour. She and John had to jump from the train into the saddle of their horses without breaking their necks.

John went first without hesitation. He landed hard against the saddle and grabbed a hold of the horn to keep from falling off. Next came Jodi. When Jed looked inside the engine room, she was throwing every bit of wood and coal she could find into the boiler. She was black from head to toe. Then she set the train to full throttle and ran two steps, and leaped onto the back of Sandy, her trusted horse. She landed perfectly, grabbed the reins, veered off and headed southwest at a gallop.

Back where the passengers waited, there was total confusion. Nobody was sure what had happened. It was apparent they stole the train and carriages. Some of the second-class passengers picked up their things and started the long walk to Harrisburg. Not dressed for the part, there was no way the rich and wealthy would walk to their destination—especially the women.

~

AT THE HARRISBURG TRAIN STATION, the boarding platform was packed. People already were trying to push their way to the front of the line so they could board first. Men stood by with large handcarts that carried the cargo or luggage of the affluent. Five boys stood in the shade of the building as they pitched pennies against the wall.

Somebody called out, "The train's coming."

"That's unusual," one would-be female passenger said. "I haven't heard the whistle announcing its arrival, especially because it is running a tad late."

When Jodi leaped from the roaring train, she had stoked the boiler as full as possible and levered the throttle to full speed. By the time the train entered the Harrisburg train station, it was going no less than twenty miles per hour. The sheer inertia of twenty-two tons of steel ran right through the station, over the emergency blockade and careened off the tracks. It slammed into another train waiting to be loaded. A cloud of dust rose so high visibility fell to zero as the boiler exploded like a firebomb. Nobody was injured, but the train was demolished. The passenger cars quickly went up in smoke, as did the cars of the second train. The train station was rendered unusable for weeks.

"What on earth?" the woman said as she saw the train roar past. A few of the women were blown off their feet by the explosion of the engine's boiler.

It took hours for anybody to figure out small bits and

pieces of what happened. The robbery of the banks was reported via telegraph and suggested the train might have been involved. The disappearance of the passengers remained a mystery, as well as who had the audacity to ram the train into the station. Since the boiler blew up, no human remains were found in the locomotive.

It took the authorities a few days to figure out what had happened and where the passengers were. They collected them with a train that wasn't damaged and brought them to Harrisburg.

Descriptions of the outlaws varied. The engineer and the brakeman could only describe a beautiful woman. Some passengers said one outlaw was White and the other Black. None of the passengers had seen the woman who abducted the train.

Everybody claimed they couldn't recognize the faces of the men. They all knew what kind of men robbed trains, and none of them wanted to get shot for the bank's money or the railroad.

At first, Jesse James was accused because his reputation made him the culprit in every robbery that took place. He was accused of every train robbery from Missouri to Oklahoma and Colorado.

CHAPTER 12

EL MOLINO

Once Rooster Beastly managed to torture every drop of information from the Lipan Apache, Chatto, he knew exactly where to go. Drop by bloody drop, he had gotten him to talk a little bit at a time. When the captain was informed of the outrageous display of brutality, he just flicked his hand at the comment as though the complainer was a fly or a bothersome insect.

Beastly had gotten what they wanted from the Indian. They couldn't set him free to warn the outlaws, though. None of the officers dared cut him down for fear of the Rooster's wrath. So, they left him for the vultures, which would make short work of him in a few days.

The following day the patrol started early, too early for most of the troop. Sergeant Beastly didn't tolerate any freeloaders among his men. Those who didn't jump right up and prepare for the day got a swift kick in the ass and extra guard duty. Beastly wasn't gentle about it either. He felt a commander who showed weaknesses wasn't fit to command men whose duty was to die for the cause. He had fought in every war he could find and sought out battles in every corner of the country. He led campaigns against many of the Indian tribes. Most of that time, he risked his life as a soldier.

Finally, when he realized his services were worth more than mere wages, he resigned and worked as a scout. Once he proved himself, he named his price, and nobody complained. When nobody else could find a target, he was the man they called. When an outlaw was too dangerous to approach, they called Rooster. He basked in the glory of shooting sassy villains and enjoyed fighting hostile Indians.

If the truth is known, Rooster was more mercenary than guide or scout. Many men made wagers on the origins of his name. Most thought he made his Christian name up himself. He certainly was a beast in battle, making the name appropriate. Nobody had the cojones to ask him, though. As the pot increased, so did the curiosity of the men. Rumors of his origins and feats ran rampant among the patrol. Tales of his brutality toward hostile Indian spread far and wide.

At times, he was brutal to sassy soldiers. His discipline was harsh. In battle, he shot more than one soldier for not standing and fighting as ordered. He tolerated little and demanded everything. He was a no-nonsense, take-no-prisoners leader with more experience than the entire patrol combined.

It took them two days to cross the desert without water. They hadn't discovered Jodi's secret watering hole, which Jed and John used. They even had a large stash of money buried there.

Captain Gash and Sergeant Beastly rode toward the small Mexican village of El Molino with thirty soldiers in formation. A giant cloud of dust followed the White warriors as they rode toward the poor settlement of Mexican peasants. A few of the residents looked at the approaching sand cloud. At first, they mistook them for the Mexican Federales. They were shocked when they saw they were gringos. What would gringo soldiers want way out in the middle of nowhere? They all knew it couldn't be a good sign. Gringo soldiers seldom were.

The town mayor calmly walked to the head of the military formation as the troop rode into the town square. They remained mounted. The spokesman for El Molino clearly wore no weapons and even smiled at the visitors to his impoverished town. He greeted them in English and with open arms, offering what little the poor village had to offer.

"Have you lost your way?" Mayor Gomez asked. "Can we offer you water? There aren't any Indians out here anymore. The land is too dry. Back twenty years, this land was rich for crops. That's what the grain mill was for." He pointed at the ruins of the windmill.

"The foundation of civilization rests upon the adherence to the law," Captain Gash said, standing in his stirrups. His words were loud enough for all to hear. "Today, we are the law."

Gomez looked back at the captain, puzzled. Then he found himself looking down the gun barrel of a giant man dressed in buckskins. His face looked like a bulldog.

"Where's them damned bushwhackers? We know they're here. So, don't you dare story me, cockroach," Beastly growled. "Before answering my question, understand your life depends on what you say. I'll squash you like a bug. I don't mess about with beaners. So, let's hear what you've got to say or die where you stand."

Mayor Gomez spoke fair English, but he didn't quite understand what the angry-looking White man asked him. He didn't understand the word bushwhackers or cockroach. Beaner, he understood and knew the defamatory meaning. He stood his ground and answered with a puzzled look. He didn't know what the US Army was doing in Mexico. The Lipan Apache moved farther away so the White people couldn't find them.

Rooster's back teeth were locked, the muscles tensed as his neck turned red with fury. Beads of sweat populated his face as a blood vessel pulsated on the side of his forehead. The report of the Colt Walker revolver rolled over them like cracking thunder. The mayor's blood spread into muddy puddles in the dirt. Smoke wafted from the barrel of the heavy gun. The hole in the city's leader's chest was the size of a fist. His eyes stared blindly at the sun.

Captain Gash drew his sword and ordered a skirmish line. As soon as his men fell into formation, he yelled, "Charge!"

They attacked and ransacked the village as if the entire Confederate army was hiding there. Men rode horses into homes, shooting every living thing in sight. The roofs of the adobe huts burned.

They rooted out the remaining villagers. They beat and tortured them for information on the rebels from Quantrill's Raiders. They knew they had to be hiding somewhere in the village.

When their efforts failed, the captain put Rooster to work. He would track the outlaws like a dog until he found them. He never failed. At least not yet, and he doubted a couple of Confederate deserters would give him too much trouble.

"Now hear this," Captain Gash said, angry as hell.

He knew the outlaws were someplace nearby. His information was fresh. Nobody could have warned them because they shot, tortured and hung the Apache with the gossip. That was why they knew he spoke the truth.

"If anybody knows about Jed Coal or a negro by the name of John Noland, speak now before it's too late," the captain ordered.

The problem was there were no more folks in town who spoke English, and none of the men with the captain knew more than Spanish vulgarities. The situation was at a stalemate. Had the captain found Quantrill's men here, he could have justified the slaughter. Now that they hadn't seen a trace of the marauders, there was but one thing to do.

Captain Gash nudged his horse spur-to-spur with Rooster's, leaned in close and whispered, "No survivors."

Then he wheeled his horse around and began to ride north again. He heard the immediate crack of weapons as he rode away angry. They had tricked him again. Was it that damned Lipan Apache, or were Coal and Noland that good? Now, there was no turning back. The gauntlet had been put in place.

The last thing they did was burn everything that remained standing to the ground. Some fires were so hot the adobe melted.

Dead bodies lay across the small village. As Rooster gazed across the killing field, he looked for any movement to make sure everybody was dead. Of course, the best way be sure was an additional headshot. He cared little; they were only Mexicans anyway.

Who cared how or why the villagers died? It may be months before somebody discovered them way out here.

The outlaws thought they could hide from Captain Gash, but they were wrong. They were closer than ever. Both officers could feel it.

Rooster Beastly rode out of the ghost town at a lope. Blood dripped from the tip of his saber. The rest of the men followed. If anybody returned to El Molino, they would find it uninhabitable. They burned all grain or food stock. They made sure the town was destroyed. All that was left was a scar on scorched earth. Capt. Gash had made his mark.

CHAPTER 13

EAGLES PASS

WHEN THE THREE OUTLAWS FINALLY MADE IT TO SOUTH Texas, they knew they were only a few days from the safety of their hideout. Although they were exhilarated, they were tired from the long journey and ready for a rest. They headed straight for the trading post. They knew better than to let anybody see them together so close to Fort Duncan. So, Jed decided to go in to see if he could scare up any news on their robbery and train heist.

They made camp far enough away so anyone wandering from the settlement wouldn't run across them by accident. John was a master at finding shooting positions that hid he and Jed from prying eyes. He applied those same skills to find them a secure campsite.

Jed's beard had grown out again, so he pulled out his shaving kit and shaved his face clean, making him harder to recognize. All the wanted posters on he and John were with his full growth of beard and shoulder-length hair. He never shaved once throughout the entire Civil War. He doubted any clever soldiers coming from Fort Duncan would be looking for a clean-shaven White man on his own. They will be looking for the men on the wanted posters. On the last flier, Jed saw it mentioned a woman, but no description was available.

"Here, give me those scissors and razor," Jodi said as her blue eyes flashed mischief. "All you're going to do is mess up your hair. This is where it's best to let a woman take charge."

Jed wanted to protest, but Jodi promptly pulled at his chin hairs and said, "Hold still or I might cut your throat. Man up, Jed. I ain't a dentist."

She skillfully snipped away with the scissors as long locks of hair vanished, and a younger version of Jed Coal emerged. She had forgotten how handsome he was under all that hair. When they first met—no, when their worlds collided—he wore a few days' growth, and his hair was short enough to see his ears. Over the months, he was reluctant to shave again, but that bearded, long-haired Rebel was the one whose face was on all the posters.

Fort Duncan was only a mile and a half away from Eagles Pass, so Jed knew soldiers could be in town. He had spent his last years fooling the enemy and was nervous about going into a village with a Yankee fort nearby.

"You know what?" Jodi asked as she finished shaving the last bit of his beard. She pinched his nose between two fingers and scraped the straight razor down until the last of his mustache was gone. "You look like another man without that scraggly beard."

"I'd say if you put on a pretty dress and go with Jed, you two could pass as a normal couple," John said as he sipped on a hot cup of coffee. "A single male stranger riding into town always gets folks' attention whether they be well shaven or not. But if you two go like you are husband and wife, I doubt anybody gives you a second glance."

Jed grumbled a bit at first, but he saw the logic. He hardly ever paid much attention to a couple walking down the streets of a town but always kept his eyes on single males or groups of men. It was there the danger lurked.

"All right, then." Jed smiled, and it reached his eyes when they locked with Jodi's. For a moment there, they stared into each other's souls. Jodi was surprised, puzzled and happy at the same time. "It sounds like a good idea. But we best get a story straight if someone gets chatty with us."

"Why not Mr. and Mrs. Goodnight?" Jodi asked. "If anybody asks any questions about the family, I got all the answers. You can play a deaf-mute, Jed."

"That shouldn't be too much of a task for Jed." John laughed.

Both Jodi and John burst out laughing at their jokes, but Jed didn't get it. The laughter was contagious, though. Soon, he was laughing too. Despite them being wanted and all, they felt good. What they just did had to be a first. Robbing two banks at the same time, then stealing the train.

The next time they crossed paths with Jesse and Frank James, they won't be happy to find out they had committed the masterful theft. They still hadn't seen a newspaper to find out how it panned out in Harrisburg station when the train didn't stop but plowed onward until there were no more tracks. They all looked forward to that bit of news.

"You best go as Mr. and Mrs. Jones," John said. "Men don't take the wife's last name."

Like many places across Texas, Jodi had been to Eagles Pass once. She and her father went to the fort nearby to sell beeves to feed the soldiers back in the day. On their way back, they took a wagon load of supplies. It was part of the payment for the cattle. Often, they bartered their beef when it was a good deal. They had to feed the ranch hands too. This had been a few years back, so she didn't know if the White man and the Indian woman still ran the trading post or not. Even if they were still there, she was much more of a young girl back then. She doubted they would remember her.

Jodi suddenly realized she was going to act like Jed's wife for just a short spell. Even if it was just for play, it gave her a funny feeling inside. It was like she was about to get a little taste of what she had dreamed. Hopefully, they would have a pleasant, uneventful day and won't end up having to kill somebody.

As John said, they looked like a couple when they rode into town. Jodi wore a skirt and rode sidesaddle. Today her riding outfit was brown and more conservative. She didn't want to draw attention like she did when she wore her white dress. She had her hair pulled back into a ponytail, and she buttoned her white shirt to the top. She looked like a wealthy rancher's wife, and Jed looked like another person. When Jodi glanced his way, she hardly recognized him. Between the haircut shaving five years from his face and his dress, Jed acted like the man she imagined he was before the war. The internal scars were gone. She was getting a glance at Jed with his guard down and not looking to kill instantly.

"Over there is the trading post where we got supplies." She read the sign: "Rick Pawless Trading Post. That's right, the owner's name is Rick, and his Indian wife is Minnie. This place is the center of information for the area. There's always Indian gossip for sale here, at least that was what my pa said. He said they knew where the Comanche were and gave us directions to stay out of trouble on our way home."

Jodi was doing all the talking, so she stepped down from Sandy and walked around, and stared Jed in the eyes.

"If you're gonna act like my husband, you best get to it," Jodi growled. "I'd never marry a mute. I like to talk too much."

To Jodi's surprise, Jed said, "Whatever you say, darlin'." He gave her his best smile and her anger vanished like a puff of smoke on a windy day.

Jodi felt her face would break; her grin was so wide. She grabbed Jed's hand in hers and said, "Come along, honey. Let's go shopping."

For Jed, her calloused hand felt dainty in his. They were nearly half the size. When he took a breath of air, scents rose from the ruffles of her dress and her hair. Suddenly her beauty astounded him. The sun shone down on her face, and it glowed when she looked up at him. His heart skipped a beat and then another.

Jodi laughed as she saw him change. She tugged at his arm as they walked toward the trading post. Jodi loved to go shopping, even in such a rough place as Eagles Pass.

Jed squinted his eyes as he peered into the darkened, smelly cantina. His eyes sifted through the small crowd of people inside, following whispers between men and women. Jodi hung her arm in his and urged him forward.

"Well, I'll be a two-tailed dog," Rick Pawless called out as soon as he saw Jodi. "My-oh-my, how you've grown, young woman. You remember me, don't cha?"

"Yes, sir, Mr. Pawless." Jodi smiled as her eyes twinkled. "This is my husband, Jed Jones."

The burly mountain man came out from behind the bar, gave Jodi an unexpected hug, and proffered his hand to Jed. Congratulations, Jed. Any friend of the Goodnights is a friend of ours.

"You've grown into a fine young woman," Minnie, Rick's wife, said as she too hugged Jodi. "How's your pa?"

"Pa passed away over a year ago," Jodi whispered.

Both Rick and Minnie frowned. Her father had treated them fair when most White men tried to cheat them because they were backwoods people.

"I'm damned sorry to hear that, Jodi," Rick said. "Your father was a fine man. Let's have a drink to your pa; may he rest in peace."

Minnie pulled out a gallon ceramic jug from under the bar and poured three fingers into each glass. It was a colorless liquid that smelled flammable. When Jodi took a sip of the harsh white lightning, she nearly choked. It lightened the mood and made all four laugh. Jodi didn't intend to have the high spirits of her day ruined. She was basking in the act of playing Jed's wife. He seemed to like it, too.

"What can I do for you two today?" Nick asked.

"You both have to stay for lunch," Minnie said. "It'll be my treat."

"If I remember right, your cookin' was mighty good, ma'am," Jodi politely replied.

"Call me Minnie just like everybody else does," the Indian woman said and smiled. "Do you like venison, Jed?"

Jed got caught off guard because, to that point, Jodi hadn't allowed him to talk. That was fine by him.

"Why, yes, ma'am," Jed said. "I'd like it just fine to supper with y'all."

"Well, I'll be," Rick said in his booming voice. "Jodi went and got herself a southern gentleman. You keep a good hold on him, girl. Manners is a hard thing to find in this part of Texas. You've done fine, girl."

"We came here to barter, Rick." Jodi grinned, proud and beaming.

"And what is it you got to trade, girl?" Minnie asked.

"I'll be right back," she said as she turned and skipped to the tavern door and disappeared outside.

She still had some of the habits of a young girl. Jed felt his heart miss another beat as he watched her go.

When she came back in, she had five coiled bullwhips hooked in the crook of her arm.

"Fine handcrafted bullwhips I made myself," Jodi said proudly.

Rick picked up one of the bullwhips and inspected it. It had a snakeskin-covered handle with a tightly woven braid that was strong and supple at the same time. At the end of the whip, the lash was supple and split like a viper's tongue. She had both snake whips and bullwhips.

"How about a cracking and target contest?" Jodi said as Rick and Minnie inspected the handcrafted working tools.

"I'll warn ya," Rick said. "I was a bullwhacker for a spell." He grinned from ear to ear."

"Well, let's go out back where I saw a clothesline,"

Jodi said, chuckling. "Bring along five pieces of paper and some clothes pegs."

Beside the old, rugged log building was a long clothesline, where sheets festooned in the breeze. Jodi selected an empty stretch of rope and pinned the pieces of paper in a line, like targets for pistol practice.

She lay the coiled assortment of bullwhips and snake whips out on the garden worktable and said, "Take your pick, Rick. You too, Jed. Be prepared to be licked by a woman."

"Ain't I allowed to play too," Minnie asked. The crafty woman knew as much about outdoor living as any White man.

Each one selected a whip, and both men stood about like a couple of tree stumps. Jodi shook her head, spat into her hands, and rubbed them together to get a better grip.

"Well, boys, if y'all ain't going to start, I reckon I will," Jodi said as she grabbed her favorite bullwhip. It was the fancy one with a snakeskin handle. She whirled it around her head a few times, making it crack, again and again, with each flick of her wrist.

Then she whirled it over her head again and lashed out at the paper, which split in two. Jed and Nick gasped in surprise. Obviously, neither one expected a White girl to use a bullwhip as good as any man they knew.

Minnie carefully felt the weight of each of the whips and selected a snake whip. She skillfully flung it back and forth, making it crack like a gunshot. She, too, split the piece of paper hanging from a clothes peg. Now the men had been called out and challenged.

"Who goes first?" Jed asked. "I never had much practice with a whip back on the farm. We used mules rather than oxen, and they be generally strong and less cranky. So, there was never any need for much more than a switch from a weeping willow tree."

"I worked as a bullwhacker on the Chisholm Trail, driving a wagon train north," big old Rick said. "The wagon trains almost always use oxen or even some mules because horses lacked the stamina and are less agreeable when pulling heavy loads. I figure I can hold my own with a whip."

He took a hold of the largest one and whirled it around his head, making it crack like thunder. He wheeled it like he did over the heads of the oxen to keep them going. He entirely missed when he took a crack at the paper fluttering on the clothesline. He was so shocked his jaw dropped, leaving his mouth open in surprise.

"I reckon crackin' a whip over an oxen's head ain't as hard as hittin' something with the lash. I missed that target by two feet."

Next, it was Jed's turn. He had no expectations because he couldn't remember ever needing to use a whip. Sure, his family had a poor dirt farm, but it was mostly cotton and hemp. They had a sturdy mule on the farm. They used that old animal for just about everything. Still, he was going to give it a try.

"Use mine, Jed," Jodi offered and whispered. "It has small lead pellets woven into the end to give it more weight."

It impressed Jed that Jodi was so knowledgeable about outdoor life. He noted her hand often had the habit of feeling for her right leg. A habit that comes with carrying a gun. Rick was beginning to believe Jodi Goodnight might have changed in the years since he saw her last. Hell, she was a little girl back then. Now, she was a full-grown woman.

Jed managed to get the long whip twirling around his head, but when he tried to lash out at the paper on the clothesline, the whip came back and cracked him instead. A dark whelp rose on his arm where the popper hit.

"I figure it's a tie between Jodi and me," Minnie said with a proud glow. She was no bigger than a corn nugget, but the Indian woman was no daisy.

CHAPTER 14

RICK PAWLESS

ONCE THE BRAGGING WAS OVER, RICK MADE A DEAL FOR all but Jodi's whip and let Minnie convince them to stay for dinner. She was known in the territory for having one of the best restaurants. They had venison and wild javelin boar with corn on the cob, mashed potatoes, and fried yucca root. She made a large pan of cornbread, and they passed around the jug of white lightning as they ate. The food was so good they hardly talked throughout the meal. Rick seemed to be in a great mood and laughed at everything. Sometimes his body convulsed with laughter, and his eyes swelled with tears.

After the bullwhip contest, Rick and Jed brooded a little over being bested by women. Especially Rick, who considered himself a mountain man in every sense of the word.

Minnie went to get dessert, and Rick ran off to the bar to check on things leaving Jed and Jodi alone for a moment.

"There's something you need to understand," Jodi said as she leaned in closer and smiled wickedly.

"Women know men lie about what they do all the time when in front of ladies. It's a given fact. So, don't be surprised if I don't believe everything you or Rick say. As a matter of fact, I figure the ones who come right off and brag about their lives are lying. The men who have the real power and courage be those who keep it to themselves." She winked at him and gave him a quick kiss on the lips.

Jodi surprised Jed again. He believed it to be a compliment, but he never really knew what to make of her, although he knew she was special. When she kissed him, he enjoyed the softness of her lips. He savored the taste by running his tongue across his lips. For the first time, he noticed the dimples on her cheeks when she was happy.

For a few seconds, they got lost in each other's eyes. It was as though they were gazing at the other's soul. Minnie returned with a peach cobbler and burst their bubble.

When Rick returned, Jed and Jodi were brought back to reality and why they came to the trading post. They wanted information. Jed mentioned a train robbery in passing. As soon as he did, Rick's eyes lit up. He loved a good bit of gossip.

"I heard the outlaws vanished into thin air," Rick said. "The train ran from where they left the passengers all the way to Harrisburg like some sort of ghost was driving it. They say it came running through the station at a fierce speed and crashed into another train before running off the rails. Lucky nobody got killed.

"The first newspaper rag to report it said it was a ghost train. Eventually, the railroad sent men out in search of the passengers. They were a bit uncomfortable when they were discovered, but nobody was injured.

"Two fellas, one Black and one White, were who done it, or so they say. You know how gossip is. By the time it gets all the way down here, it's exaggerated some. The newspaper said it took them near on four days to figure out what the hell happened. They still ain't all that sure. But they did figure out who did it. The outlaws must have been so far away they didn't even take chase by then. But they did put their pictures in the newspapers. I've got a copy at the bar. Ya wanna look?"

The color drained from Jed's face. Lucky for him, Nick didn't notice. He quickly regained his composure. Jodi squeezed his arm and looked at him with apprehension in her eyes. Their happy little ruse might have been uncovered. Jed wondered if he would have to kill Rick, something he'd hate but might be compelled to do.

When Rick came with the newspaper, the picture was right in the middle of the front page. It was the old photograph from when Jed and John were still with Quantrill's Raiders. John's sketch was clear, but the bearded man next to him looked very little like the clean-shaven man with whom Rick shared a meal. Jed's eyes, often hallow and empty, were quite different in person. They couldn't be duplicated on a piece of paper.

"They look like a couple of dangerous outlaws," Jodi said, faking shock. "Especially the bearded fella. He looks like a wild animal."

Jed kicked her shin under the table, but Jodi just smiled.

"We're lucky out here there ain't such folks about," their host added.

"Oh, wicked men come here to Eagles Pass too,"

Minnie said. "All of 'em ain't outlaws. There was just that type of men here a few days back. They were Army, all but one. He was an Indian killer."

"What did they want, I wonder," Jodi said, trying not to act too curious.

"Some said they were after Apache," Rick replied. "Others said they were hunting Confederates criminals. I had little to do with them myself. I don't get on well with Army types, especially when they be Yankees. This officer talked all snobby like he was from someplace back East, like Boston."

Jed folded the newspaper over, so his likeness wasn't staring at him. He did what he always did when danger was near; he acted calm and cool. He didn't want to ask any more questions of the couple for fear of raising suspicion. He knew, though, if he and John were seen together, the jig would be up.

Minnie cleared the table with the help of a young Indian woman, and Rick went back to tend to the bar, leaving Jed and Jodi alone again. But now, their minds no longer were on their carnal cravings but on survival.

"The Army was looking for us," Jed said. "I wonder if they got a fix on El Molino? If there were Indian killers with them, it might have gone poorly for the Mexican folks in town."

Neither Jed nor Jodi noticed two Indians walk into the room. They were suddenly both standing behind them. Startled, Jed went for his pistol, but a large knife was up against his throat so quickly he couldn't understand how the Tonkawa Indian moved so fast.

"We don't come here to harm you," Potak said as Tuc removed the knife from Jed's throat. "If we wanted to kill you, we would've done so before you left the Black man back where he thinks he hides unseen. I'm surprised Black people are at times as foolish as White people. I thought they would be more like red men. Perhaps I have more to learn."

The tension in Jed's face relaxed, but Jodi was having difficulty sitting still in the presence of such a terrifying Indian warrior. Hell, it even gave Jed the willies when he looked into Tuc's eyes. He thought Jesse James had dangerous-looking eyes, but the Indians were something else again.

"Why are you following us?" Jed asked, now on the defensive. He felt the danger and was careful what he said.

"We hoped you would pass by sooner, but you both took a long time to ride from Harrisburg." Potak chuckled. "Don't be alarmed. You're Jodi Goodnight, ain't ya?"

"Yes, I am," Jodi said, but her voice was empty. She was more scared than she was when they stole the train.

"Tuc and I are friends of your uncle, Charles Goodnight, and his pard, Oliver Loving," Potak said with compassion. "We aim you no harm. We have been waiting to warn you."

"How do you know my uncle?" Jodi asked.

"Everybody knows your uncle," Tuc said, his mouth an emotionless gash.

"We've worked for Goodnight as scouts. Wherever Goodnight goes, so does Oliver Loving. We may go with them to Montana if they ever make up their minds. I, too, would like to see the Northern Plains. They have been talking about it for years," Potak explained.

"Now that you know so much about us, I reckon you know who the Black fella and I are, doncha?" Jed asked.

The look in the White man's eyes changed as

suddenly as a lightning bug flashes. The Tonkawa scouts, saw it, even though Jodi didn't.

"We don't care what White men do to each other," Tuc said in a whisper. "Many Indians hoped you would kill each other off when you went to war. Indians never suffered such losses and continue. Now, all the men who are left are haunted by war. Men like me are made for this way of life, and I think you are too. Others suffer the experience but never become true warriors. You have many enemies. Some of those enemies are our enemies, too. So, if we help you find them, we will all be pleased."

"And who are these mutual enemies we got?" Jed said as he neared his head and lowered his voice.

"A sergeant called Rooster," Potak replied. "He's an Indian killer from the war with the northern tribes. He's an evil man. His captain's named Gash. They are not looking for Apache like most army patrols. They came here looking for a White man and a Black man from Missouri."

Jed waited. He knew there was more to come. Deep in his gut, he knew what they were going to say. He glanced at Jodi. She still hadn't connected the dots.

"They bought some gossip from a Lipan Apache, named Chatto. He was known to be foolish. They were supposed to speak to my cousin and me."

The revelation startled Jed, but he regained his composure. His muscles tensed.

"And why you two? Jed asked.

"We sell gossip, but only the gossip we wish to sell. Chatto should have known what would happen."

"Where is Chatto now?" Jed asked. "I want to talk to him at once."

"You will have to go on a long journey if you want to

see Chatto, and I am afraid you cannot come back," Potak said.

"What are you talking about?" Jed asked, now losing patience.

"He was shot, burned, stabbed, finally hung and left for the vultures," Tuc replied as he stared deep into the White man's eyes. He saw he was a true warrior, like the Tonkawa. The scary brave nodded his head. "It was done right behind the fort. He's still there; we can so see him."

"What did this Chatto tell the soldiers?" Jed asked, but he already knew.

"He said you were in the Mexican village of El Molino."

Silence came over the four. Minnie returned, but she acted like she already knew all about what they talked about. Tuc and Potak were not bothered by her presence.

"Minnie is Indian, as we are. Her tribe is one of the few we are not at war with," Potak said. "It was she who told us about Chatto."

"Did the soldiers come back through here?" Jodi asked, frightened by what the answer might be.

"They did," Minnie said. "I heard them say they were going to ride to Harrisburg."

"And El Molino?" Jodi asked.

"I don't know," Potak said. "We will ride with you and see. The Mexican peasants in El Molino were our friends, too."

"Do the pair of you know everybody in Texas?" Jed asked, not hiding his sarcasm.

Potak chuckled and said, "When you travel all the time, the world becomes smaller. You eventually meet and learn of all people. We know you, you know Minnie, she knew Chatto and on and on. In the end, we are not as many as you believe. Since the White men came, we are many more people, but the land is the same size. Soon we will be far too many."

They heard the clomping of boots on the porch of the trading post, finally casting shadows under the closed door of the dining room.

The Indians suddenly disappeared into the shadows. Jed and Jodi waited behind the door with their pistols in hand. She pressed her back into him. It made her feel safe.

She looked at him wide-eyed. "What now?"

They heard a commotion outside the door then they heard Rick Pawless shout, "Nobody walks into my home without an invitation."

They heard the click of the hammer on an old flint-lock. Finally, the boot steps faded, and Rick returned. Pawless looked into the shadow, where he knew the scouts stood. He added, "You two best take these folks to El Molino. The soldier boys got riled up about something. It's best if y'all don't hang around and find out what it is or ain't."

AFTER MEETING with the Tonkawa at Eagles Pass, the three outlaws struck out toward El Molino. The Indians said they would go with them, but they disappeared before the first hour passed. One minute they were riding beside them, and the next, they vanished into thin air. It spooked Jed. They knew they would be too late to save the villagers. Still, there was no turning back.

From the village, they hoped they would be able to track the soldiers who were hunting them. Had they known the US Army would break international law and ride two days south of the border, they would have never jeopardized the village. They would have fled farther south.

Now they feared they might have cost some of them their lives. Hopefully, the injured and damage would be limited. It would take less than twenty minutes for a patrol to see they weren't there, and as they always made it a point to travel with all their valuables and clothing, there was no trace of them left.

Jed spoke as much to himself as to the others. "We got two possible scenarios. One is they roughed up a couple of village folks and searched the town. When they saw we weren't there, they went on their way, following our track back north. If I know anything about the Yankee soldiers who hunt down Rebels, though, they may have tortured or killed some folks in town."

He paused and then added, "We'll be finding out soon enough."

Jed went silent and kept his eyes glued to the sky to the south.

That night they decided to make camp just before the sun set at the water hole, a day's ride from El Molino. It was one of the hottest days of the year, and they decided not to chance the arid desert. When they got there, they found the two strange Indians sitting under a scraggly tree that provided them just enough shade. They stared as if hypnotized by the sunset. None of them remembered a tree being there when they visited before.

When the party stepped down, the medicine man held up his hand for them to remain silent. They watched the sunset with such intensity they found it odd. A prism of colors ended the day. Not until the last ray of sun left their faces did Tonkawa turn to address the trio.

"I been here several times, and I don't remember seeing any tree here," John said as he eyed the Indians suspiciously.

Potak smiled and said, "Maybe we are just lucky, and it followed us here."

They all knew Indians were oddly different. Jodi had more contact with them in Texas but dealt mainly with the treacherous Comanche. She watched her back, even though the scouts seemed to share their interest. They were so odd in their actions; she couldn't help but be scared. They were so unsettling, she became uncertain of her own beliefs. For man, the unknown was the most terrifying. Indians knew this.

Shortly after they arrived, the Tonkawa ate salted pork and beans and quickly fell asleep. From the moment they lay on their blankets, they began to snore. She believed they could sleep anywhere.

When they awoke the following day, the Indians were gone again. Jed and Jodi checked around the water hole but found no tracks or signs of anyone else but them. John cleaned the camp and began to saddle the horses. The village was still a day's ride away.

As they rode in silence, Jed didn't show any emotion. Jodi got the feeling he was expecting the worst. She pulled her pistol, checked the chambers and looped the tie over the hammer when she slipped it back into the holster. She kept her eyes glued to the sky before them. She had been with Jed and John for long enough to know to look for vultures.

"We best bury the money by the spring on the way back," Jodi said. "We can't go traipsing around the country with sacks full of money. I don't even know how much we got. I didn't want to bury it with the Indians around."

"Do you think we can do something without them finding out?" John asked. "Black folks got names for people like them. They see the future and can cast the evil eye. They can talk to ghosts too. At least that's what my mammy used to say."

"Does it matter now?" Jed asked. He had that faraway look in his eyes again. She knew he would not stop until he got revenge if they found what they suspected. Jed didn't have a superstitious bone in his body; he dealt only with facts.

Now, he was hell-bent on checking on the village. Then, he would hunt this Rooster character down and kill him.

CHAPTER 15

ROOSTER TAIL

THE ONLY SOUND WAS THE CLOPPING OF HORSES' HOOVES as they echoed in the night. Later the coyotes sang their nightly choruses.

When the crescent moon rose to their left, it cast dim silver shadows on the right side of the riders. Jodi was nodding in the saddle as she dozed off and on. Jed and John could travel for days without sleep. John's father had taught him to make a mix of herbs that allowed them to walk all day and stay up all night. It abated fatigue and erased their hunger.

John claimed his father brought the concoction with him on the slave ship that brought them from Africa. John grew the plants in his backyard back on the plantation. The bushes had bright green leaves but now were dry and brittle. They sprinkled ground charcoal, folded it in the leaf, and chewed on the plugs. Every hour or so, they made up a new plug to chew. Jed never understood where the plants came from, but they worked when the war demanded they stay awake for days on end. Sleep was often a luxury during the Civil War.

With the first hint of light, they immediately saw the vultures in the sky. Jed squinted under the brim of his hat and gazed into the distance. There appeared to be hundreds of scavengers, if not more. It was like a lazy black cloud turning around and around over El Molino. Jed nudged the flanks of his horse and brought him to a trot. His heart was thundering, but his mind was clear. Everything smelled like blood—or something rotten and swampy. The sun wasn't up yet, and the bodies were already beginning to bloat. Lonely chimneys stood as monuments of burned-out homes.

Jodi tried to hide her shock and how she felt. Two lines showed up around her mouth like parentheses.

"Lord have mercy," she huffed. "Happiness runs from us like a scalded dog."

Jed rode from house to house as John took cover and kept his Henry rifle leveled for protection if he saw something out of order. But the town was as still as a cemetery. Hell, it was a cemetery. Everyone was dead.

When Jodi looked over at John, tears ran down his cheeks as he stared straight ahead at something far beyond her vision. She tried to cover her surprise to see a grown man cry. She figured John was crying about his family and what might have happened to them when the Army looked for them. Everywhere they turned, they brought death.

When Jed finished, he didn't say a word. All he did was exchange looks with John. The Black scout nodded. Jed looked carefully at the calvary's tracks as John stepped down and began pointing out differences in how they stepped or scuffed a hoof. They both looked at Jodi, but they knew better than ask. They knew she would insist on going with them.

Their escape from the war had turned into a plague, spreading a fatal infection to everyone they met. Her heart was now kicking at the inside of her chest.

For the hundredth time in the last two days, John felt sure someone was behind them. He knew it had to be the Indians. Soldiers would never have so much patience. Before he could turn around, the scouts appeared from nowhere.

"How'd you get here before us?" Jed asked.

They both sat down in the shade of the ugly little tree. John's brain squirmed. He always thought he was the best tracker west of the Missouri River. It looked like he wasn't.

"The Blue Coats killed the people you're looking for. I think they only wanted you two—the White and Black men. I haven't heard much about the woman. She should be careful about who she tells her name to, though."

Potak struck up a conversation with them like they'd been together the entire day. He certainly didn't show any fear toward the three outlaws.

"You're a pretty good tracker," Potak said to John. "You track almost like an Indian. Most Indians would miss your track. Me, I can track ghosts, so humans are easy."

"Did you see who did it?" Jed asked.

"We saw," Tuc replied, but his face was impossible to read. "A captain and the Indian killer known as Rooster. They have a patrol of twenty-eight Blue Coats. There is no one innocent among these men. They come from the war and continue with the violence. They did this in the name of their laws and what they call justice. These laws they claim they follow were written by liars and cowards. I will ride with you. My cousin can track the devil. Today we have several to kill."

Jed had a second look at the Tonkawa Indian. He wore six or seven scalps sewn into his shirt. Jodi put on a brave face, but she couldn't make eye contact with Tuc. She refused to even admit she was scared. She shifted closer to Jed until she was pressing into him.

Whether the Army ran for the American border or would turn and fight remained unknown. They were aware of Jed and John's skills.

Rooster was the man Jed wanted for himself. If they did turn when they came into range, John would open up with his Henry rifle. If and when they get into Jodi's pistol range, it would be a free-for-all to see who lived and died. None of the three would let this slaughter go unavenged. There was no turning back.

All three of them felt responsible for the deaths of these poor Mexican peasants. "Had we realized how wanted we were, we would have made other plans," John said.

"Hindsight doesn't do shit for what's to come," Jed said. "I'm gonna kill every Yankee that was in El Molino, and for the commander and officers, I intended something special."

He'd had it with running from a war that was already over. It just seemed to carry on for him. It was time to stand and fight again. Hopefully, this would be the last of it. Win or lose; they were in it one hundred percent.

THE CLOUD of dust from thirty horses, plus extra mounts, was impossible to hide. These men rode like they owned the country and cared little who they offended. Captain Gash was sure the Mexican Federales would not confront a force of thirty trained American soldiers, even if they were trespassing on foreign soil.

The five riders following them spread out, so they kept their dust cloud down. The sun had dried the dirt into a fine powder that exploded with each fall of the horses' hooves. The Indians rode ponies that seemed to leave little dust behind. Then again, nothing was ordinary about the two young Tonkawa. At least they appeared to be on their side.

They quickly found a clear field of fire, and Jed dismounted and sat up his rifle support. He opened the breach and slid a bullet home. He wiped the sweat out of his eyes with the sleeves of his shirt; then he stared down the barrel and rifle scope.

Jed let out his breath, slipped his finger into the trigger guard and released the safety. He took a final look through the scope, leading the target a tad. When he caressed the hair trigger, a deafening report rang out as the smoke and fire chased the lead bullet out of the barrel beyond the speed of light. The last Yankee cavalryman slammed forward onto the pommel of his saddle like someone hit in the back with the flat of a shovel.

He'd already reloaded the gun and aimed at a man at the head of the column. Jed could barely make out stripes on his sleeve. He pulled the trigger again, and this shot took the soldier's arm off high in the bicep. Jed moved to the next target as he knew the man with no arm would bleed out before anyone could do anything.

Somebody in the patrol knew what they were doing. They called a retreat and sped out of rifle range. Jed took a bead on the last soldier's horse. The rider tumbled to the ground, and Jed took his final shot. He hit the running soldier in the back as he raced for cover.

He and John collected their things without a word, mounted up again, and began to ride. Jed knew this would only last for so long. He would follow them and kill more, all if he had to on his own. So far, he had killed three, ten percent of their men, in seconds. He felt it in his soul he had to make restitution for the lives of a Mexican village. Hell, they weren't even involved in the Civil War or knew where Missouri was.

That night they stopped to water the horses. Once they refreshed their animals and themselves, they turned north again and rode on into the night. If they didn't stop, they should have their campsite in sight by daylight.

The sky to the east blushed red as blood as the sun peeked over the edge of the earth. It was as if it was checking to see if it was safe before it rose farther. The last trace of stars vanished in the western heavens as a blue canvass stretched from horizon to horizon.

The calvary unit was careful and found high ground for its camp. The five who followed made a cold camp when they came upon their hiding spot. Six men held guard around the small compound. The rest of the men appeared to be asleep. They had ridden hard all the way from El Molino and now were being chased by the best sniper in the Confederate army. They knew they had to be careful.

"Hide the horses and wait here," Tuc said as he put a knife between his teeth and disappeared into the shadows of night. The moon had yet to rise, so it wasn't easy to make out objects unless they moved. Even then, the Tonkawa warrior was invisible. Jed followed him with the scope, but he saw no dark outlines.

Jodi took the horses down a gorge and hobbled them. Then she hurried back. Being out there in the dark scared the hell out of her, but she steeled to the task. She wasn't going to be the weak link in the chain.

Jed aimed his gun toward the Yankee soldiers. He could make out the boundaries in the starlight, but there was no way he could start to shoot until the moon climbed into the sky in a few hours.

A couple of hours later, Tuc returned. Jed saw his dark outline before his face because he moved without making a sound. He had a handful of fresh scalps in his fist. In the other, he held his bloody knife.

"Now there are no guards," Tuc said. He kind of smiled, but it looked more frightening than before. Jodi again turned away; she couldn't look at the scalps.

Jed and John exchanged knowing looks. They had seen such things done during the Civil War. They saw men take scalps, ears, fingers, and tongues. Men's minds change with so much violence. Once civilized, they regress to barbarians. War was hell, and they had been there and back.

By the time the moon began to shine to the east, casting bright silver light across the land, the Army camp was in turmoil. They must have discovered the guards, scalped and with their throats slit. Men were running around the camp in a panic. Jed watched them from afar. In the center, he saw a man in buckskins pull a revolver and fire a round off into the sky. The men frantically moving about suddenly stopped in their tracks. An officer exited a small tent and spoke to his troops. Jed wondered what he was saying. He, too, was angry. He saw the dead bodies in a row in the middle of the camp.

Jed knew the shot was tricky—it was just over seven hundred yards. He closed his eyes and cleared his mind of all thought and tension. He took three deep breaths blowing the air out slowly through his nose. When he opened his eye and looked down the scope at the US Army captain, he was still in his white shirt and red suspenders. He was berating the soldiers

Jed imagined how the Indian killed the guards, without warning and without awakening anyone. He had never seen anything like it, even in the war.

The soldiers were scurrying around, getting their gear to saddle up and ride north fast. Jed pulled the trigger. He felt the hard recoil, and the scope jumped before his eye. When he looked back, the bullet had just arrived. Captain Gash's shirt exploded into a bright red. The impact slammed him to the ground like he'd been hit in the chest by a sledgehammer. Rooster dove for the cover of rocks. Jed knew where he was, though, and he had him pinned down.

One by one, the sniper and spotter began their pattern. They started with the soldiers closest to the perimeter. They were the most likely to run. Taking them out first made it harder to flee for the rest of the men bunched up.

Jodi watched in shock. The Tonkawa Indians simply watched as if the theater of life and death was playing out before their eyes. They were the observers. Jodi began to tremble with fear. Her fear was not coming from the men who sought to kill them, but for what they all had become.

Finally, Jed rolled over on his back and took a deep

breath. He pulled off his bandana and wiped the sweat off his face and out of his eyes.

He passed his Sharps rifle to John and said, "I have one last thing to take care of myself."

He turned and walked out of the camp, pulling each revolver before he slipped them back into place. He wore them in the cross-draw fashion fancied by the Texas Rangers. Not many people had ever seen Jed shoot a revolver. He did almost all his work with a rifle. Only John knew. Now, it was time to see just how good Sgt. Rooster Beastly was.

He walked right down to the camp without taking any precautions. He knew if Rooster tried to get a shot off at him, John would have him dead to rights in his sights, and he would be a dead man. Jed didn't intend to give him a chance to test his skills. John knew even if Jed failed, he would shoot and kill Rooster. Either way, his days were over.

"You can stand up now, Rooster," Jed said. "I hear you been lookin' for me."

"Yeah, I stand up, and that slave of yours shoots me dead," Rooster growled back.

"You're dead either way," Jed said. "John is my friend and not my slave. All I'm doing is giving you the chance to kill me before you die, and die you will. There's a bullet with your name on it, and it's either in my pistol or in the Sharps rifle in John's hands back there some seven hundred yards.

"He can't hit me from that far," Rooster called out.

"Try him out," Jed replied. "This is your last chance, you red-legged Jayhawker. I know what you were from way back. When I heard the name Rooster, it got me wondering. When they said your last name was Beastly, it threw me off. You be one of those uppity Yankees that moved to Kansas just to kill innocent folks. Well, now you've found your bushwhacker, Rooster Johnson. I remember who you were, and I know what you've become."

Rooster stood, pulled off his hat and dusted off his clothes. He didn't seem frightened at all. On the contrary, Jed could smell his arrogance.

"I heard you be a sharpshooter with a rifle, but now we'll fight like men," Rooster taunted. "Not like women hiding behind a rock to shoot folks from afar. We'll shoot with pistols and see who's good at what. I know there ain't a Johnny Reb that can outdraw me."

Jed Coal's rifle skills were common knowledge in Missouri and Kansas. Even the marshals and sheriffs in Texas were warned not to get in a position to be bush-whacked because Jed never missed. What few knew was that when he drew his pistols, it was like a blur. At such close range, Jed could shoot the whiskers off a fly.

The sniper drew so fast Rooster didn't even get a good grip on the handle of his pistol. He blew his thumb off as the soldier tried to thumb the hammer on his revolver. When Rooster screamed, holding his damaged hand in his left, Jed shot four more times. The shots were so quick, they sounded like one roar. Four more digits fell to the dirt as blood squirted from the stubs. Now the sergeant was missing seven fingers.

The Indian killer blinked in disbelief.

Jed pulled back the hammer one last time. The chamber turned to his final bullet. He pulled the trigger, and at such range, the heavy powered revolver blew a hole the size of a silver dollar in the sergeant's chest. It came out his back the size of a cantaloupe.

The fabric around the entry wound caught fire and smoked. The smell of cordite filled the air.

"You snake-eyed, whistle-blowin', pot-bellied wind-bag. Let's hear ya talk now," Jed said as he bent over the body. He cut the scalps from his shirt, stuffed them in his mouth, and spat on him.

Later, he and John hung the body from his neck on a giant cactus and pinned a note to his chest:

WOMAN AND CHILD BUTCHER!

The other soldiers lay where they died. Only the captain remained alive, but barely. How he was still breathing after such a gunshot wound from a buffalo round surprised Jed. Then again, he'd been surprised a lot lately. He walked over to the captain, kneeled and looked him in the eyes.

"Was it worth it, Captain?" Jed asked the dying man. "You stupid bastard. The war's over."

The Tonkawa Indians caught a couple of the soldiers hiding in a ditch, and Tuc poked their eyes out and removed their tongues. They could no longer speak or see. The last thing they saw was Tuc's fierce face. It was painted for war and terrifying. The damaged soldiers were left to wander the wilderness. Maybe somebody would find them, but they couldn't identify anybody anymore.

They stopped at the spring for water and buried their money. Who didn't care if the Tonkawa saw them or not? They disappeared again right after Jed killed Rooster. He was sure they were there watching, though. He could somehow feel their presence.

Jed turned and headed back to where John and Jodi

waited on him. She tended to the horses, Jed scrounged up some firewood, and John began to prepare their supper. They seemed to be trying to occupy themselves and not to think about what had just happened. Nobody felt like talking, so they passed the evening in intense silence. You could cut the tension with a knife. They made up a quick meal, drank two pots of coffee.

Still, they all fell into a deep sleep. They were too tired after the long chase to even keep a guard. In minutes the three were snoring.

CHAPTER 16

ALONE AT LAST

JED AND JODI TOOK OFF FOR A FEW DAYS TO BE ALONE after all the violence. She knew Jed needed it, and she did too. In the last months, she had experienced more than most folks do in a lifetime. They intended to spend some quality time alone where no one could find them—not the Army or any kind of lawman or bounty hunter. They didn't even want to be bothered by their only real friend, John Noland.

The flames slipped around the logs, caressing them like long fingers. Heat radiated from the blaze as the fire's shadows danced on the walls. They were in an abandoned log cabin. It was in a hidden valley—lush and green. After being in south Texas, it was a welcomed change. As soon as Jodi got close to Jed, her heart flip-flopped—in a rush at first. She felt feverish.

Jed threw blankets on the bare wood floor before the fire. Their saddles lay as pillows at the ends. A wavering slice of moon showed through the glass, spilling silver shadows into the room. The fire crackled and popped as steam hissed from the green wood.

Outside, beads of dew formed on the green leaves and dripped onto the ground. Then it began to rain—at first just a sprinkle, then drops hit the water puddles like little bombs. Soon the drizzle turned into a downpour. Trickles of water turned to streams and were now on the verge of being a river. Jed and Jodi were warm and dry beside the fire. Jed was making some biscuits, and Jodi forked two potatoes with a stick and was baking them over the coals.

Sandy, Jodi's mare, stood out of the rain under the lean-to attached to the cabin. Jed's war-horse towered over her. She twitched her ears as she attempted to rid herself of flies and shivered her coat. Dust floated in the air like horsehide from the mare's shoulders. The horses' backs shined where the blankets made them sweat.

"Do you think we'll ever live a normal life?" Jodi asked, almost sad.

"It may not be a normal life, but it'll be a life," Jed replied as he neared his face to hers and looked into her eyes. The fire made his blue eyes turn emerald, green, like those of a cat. "That's a hell of a lot more than we had before. Being wanted is what I was during the whole war. Half the country wanted to see us Rebels dead, and we all had bounties on our heads. Now we've only got a few stragglers left after us. I reckon with time, it'll get easier."

"If they don't catch us and hang us first."

"Nobody is gonna hang you or me, darlin'," Jed promised. "If we go out—we'll go out together. With our boots on and our guns barking up a storm."

When Jed talked of life and death, he spoke like both were his long-lasting friends. He seemed to value one as much as the other. Jodi wondered if he was a religious man. Then again, not many men from the war were religious. They may have started that way but by the end, all they believed in was the wickedness of man.

Jed watched Jodi's profile. It glowed orange from the coals. With one hand, she unpinned her hair and flicked her head, making it drop over her shoulders and to her waist. Jed knew she didn't think he was watching. He studied every detail of her outline against the fire. He felt a warm glow in his stomach and, for him—an unusual calm. At that moment, it seemed his demons had faded away. Or maybe Jodi had made him forget them.

They ate in comfortable silence before the roaring hearth. Their everyday life seemed so fast and rushed. Right then, they wanted the night to last forever. If they could, they would stop time at that very moment.

Jodi leaned on her right hand and turned to Jed—her lips slightly parted. The pink of her tongue contrasted against her white teeth. Again, Jed saw her dimples when she smiled. He smiled, too.

"Are you going to wait all night or are ya gonna kiss me?" she asked. "I ain't wantin' to get married, Jed. All I want is you to love me back. Is that so much to ask?"

Jed didn't answer—Jodi hadn't expected him to. He just wasn't like that. But he did lean in and kiss her deeply, showing her how he felt. Above, thunder roared, and lightning flashed in the window, making the warm, dry comfort of the cabin all the better. They spent the night there by the fire. Jed would add another log every couple of hours, waking Jodi up and re-igniting their passion.

In the end, they spent half the night awake. They cuddled under their blankets and finally slept soundly by the fire. For them, there was only now there was no tomorrow. Living in the *now* momentarily freed them from their haunting pasts and fueled their expectations. Short moments of peace gave them hope for what appeared to be an impossible future.

Outside, a big raccoon trundled across the creek bed and stopped to smell the air. Then, it turned and scurried back the way it came. It didn't seem to mind the rain.

JOHN DECIDED to spend some time in the City of El Paso. When they split up, they weren't far away. He decided he wanted to see what it was like for a Black man to live as a free being in a city. Jed said many White people thought all Black folks looked the same, just like all Chinese looked the same for Black folks. He figured it must be the same all over. He didn't know why, but he'd heard it said. It made him feel safer; especially now that he was dressed as a gentleman. He hardly looked like the slave that fought for Capt. Quantrill and Bloody Bill Anderson.

John enjoyed his new life and his new name, John Washington. Nobody noticed him in his fancy duds. He still carried his guns, but he kept them under his coat. Some White men didn't like seeing Black men flaunting both money and weapons. It made them nervous—or maybe it was guilt or jealousy.

John was discreet as he explored the city as a free man on his own for the first time in his fifty years. He never believed it would happen or that he would break away from an owner who expected him to tend to every beck and call.

To be honest, he did feel a little strange, though. He had ridden with Jed Coal for close to five years. This was the first time they had spent any time apart. During the Civil War, they were joined as a sniper team at the hip. They had each other's back in every situation. He wondered if the war was really over for them.

As far as he could see, in El Paso, there was little law anyway. Sure, there was a town marshal, but he was drunk most of the time and responsible for half the shootings. They didn't call the city the six-gun capital of the west for nothing. It was nice being in a place where he didn't know anybody, and nobody knew him. Being infamous was not what he had expected in life, but there it was—he and everyone who rode with Captain Quantrill were marked men. Maybe he could hide out in plain sight, as Jodi said.

He was in one of the better establishments in town, one that permitted colored folks entry if they had money. It just so happened Mr. John Washington did have cash. He felt lucky, too.

He sat with his back to the corner, a habit he'd picked up riding with Captain Quantrill. He had a fine bottle of Kentucky bourbon and a half glass he sipped on. He looked into the glass as he swirled the spirits. A fat Cuban cigar rolled between his thumb and finger. He ran the length of the cigar just under his nose and inhaled. He pulled out his pocketknife, neatly cut the end off, put it between his lips and scraped a match across the tabletop. The flame infused life into the Havana as a thick cloud of smoke partially obscured his face.

He wondered what they would do next. Maybe he just might stay in El Paso for a spell. It would take him a few years to spend his part of the money they stolen. He just might take some time off. He liked being free. It wasn't anything like he expected. Actually, he didn't know what to expect. To be honest, he never thought he and Jed would survive the war. There was a passel of close calls, but Jed was always steady as a rock. He seemed impressed with his opponents' skills and trod carefully, never taking them for granted. That, in part, was what kept them alive. Of course, John's skills as a tracker allowed them to strike and vanish quickly.

Sometimes John thought Jed risked his life needlessly, as if he didn't care if he lived or died. He believed he was more careful when he felt he had to protect his spotter, John. They were all on close terms with death. They saw it every day. For men like them, your partner became your family, like a brother or sister.

El Paso was a rough and rowdy town, but John was no daisy. Only he knew how many men's lives he had taken before, during and after the war. Jed refused to count the corpses, and John couldn't help but count them.

There was movement at the bat-wing doors. Everyone's eyes turned to the newcomers. There weren't many men who made John Noland uneasy, and one of them just walked into the saloon. He was followed closely by his brother Frank James.

John picked his drink up with his left hand and rested his right under the table near his gun. He peered over the edge of the glass as he stared at his wartime companions. At first, they didn't notice their old pal from Quantrill's Raiders. They appeared to be waiting for someone else. That somebody else walked into the saloon a couple of minutes later. It was Cole Younger.

John was not one to hide from men he fought or rode

with. He put his feelings aside, but still, he kept his eye on Jesse. He had no concern with Cole or Frank, but Jesse had surprised them all on numerous occasions. If you caught him at the wrong time, you never knew what he might do. John had seen him shoot unarmed Yankees in cold blood. As the three huddled together, he knew it was just a matter of time before they noticed him.

Immediately, John decided he wouldn't relax in El Paso after all. It would be interesting to see what Jed had to say when he got back. The James Gang was in Texas for some reason. If Jesse was the leader, they were up to no good. Jesse's eyes felt John's upon him like a beacon of light at sea. Like a wild animal, he could scent and feel his surroundings. When their eyes made contact, there was a moment of hesitation.

Then, Jesse smiled and said, "I'll be damned, boys. Lookee over there. It's John, the captain's scout, all dressed up."

Jesse walked toward his table and said, "My, don't you clean up fine, John." This time his smile reached his eyes.

John stood and the four men shook hands all around. They all fought for years for the cause. The only difference was John was Black and ordered to work for Captain Quantrill. The James and Younger brothers believed states had the right to enslave people. The James brothers volunteered for the Black Flag Raiders. Younger was a regular soldier.

"I read about a bunch of outlaws claiming to be me, who robbed a paddleboat casino," Jesse said, his smile growing wide. "That was you three, wasn't it?"

"That was a case of mistaken identity, Jesse," John said. His face was impossible to read. "Some fool said the name Jesse James and the folks in the casino thought we were your gang. You would have busted a gut laughing at how those folks tamed down in three seconds. Nobody lifted a finger to stop us; they were too afraid of the James Gang." John chuckled as he remembered the incident. "It didn't seem so funny at the time, though."

"Don't worry, pard." Jesse chuckled. "I've been accused of robbing banks from her to Canada and all in the same week. It seems like half the robberies across the west are blamed on me."

"Did you hear about the two banks and the stolen train?" John whispered as the men sat at the table and huddled together so nobody else could hear.

"Nah, that couldn't have been y'all," Frank James said. "I bet it was that woman Jed's fancy on, wasn't it? She's a clever one, she is. We've been working on robbing our first train, but I never thought about stealing the whole damned thing. That's smart thinking, John."

John looked at the men he sat with, and he remembered he was just like them, only Black. Sure, Jesse was a particular type of ornery, but John had to admit he wasn't much better in the past.

John knew paranoia was a poor roommate and one dangerous bastard to be cooped up with. So, he swallowed his concern and had a drink with his old war partners. He now knew he would not linger in El Paso. He would head for the meeting place Jodi chose for them. Four of Quantrill's Raiders in the same town couldn't be a good thing. Sooner or later, someone was bound to recognize one of the four. Their faces were plastered across the country in marshal's offices and all the frontier forts.

THE DESERT MOON shone silver across the crater-filled landscape. No one appeared to live in this faraway place. Shadows shifted from west to east as the glowing orb crossed the heavens. Suddenly, two faces appeared as they bathed in the white glow. Both Tonkawa were as still as stones. They knew predators looked for motion. They waited for their prey.

When they talked, their voices were no louder than a gentle breeze. "What do you think will happen to the Black man, White man, and woman? Many confused people are coming from the north, and many dangerous men are drifting toward Texas."

"Texas has always had its fair share of dangerous men," Potak replied. "Are these men more dangerous than Comanche? I think not. If the Comanche and the Apache had the White men's weapons, they would have driven them far away ten winters ago. As for the curious trio, I think we should follow them to see what they do. I find them amusing. Maybe we can get some new gossip, too."

"We've made good money lately," Tuc said. "The Army paid us fifty dollars. We would have done it for ten. Did you see the eyes of the Long Knife when I talked to him? I never tire of watching White people who scare so easily. I hardly even tried. I would like to scare him on a dark night with my war paint. Maybe his heart would stop."

"We better not make trouble with the Blue Coats," Potak said. "They always have work for us and pay better than the Texas Rangers."

"But the Rangers are warriors like we us," Tuc said. "I would rather fight with a true warrior than someone sent from Washington. Often as not, their missions are those of fools, and half of them get killed."

"I must admit," Potak said, "the US Army teaches their officers to lie very well. They promise the Indians everything but never keep their word. Perhaps they are cleverer than us. We always see them as fools. Perhaps we are the fools and not the White men."

"We are like time," Tuc replied. "We live now, not tomorrow or yesterday. For us, time is endless."

Sometimes the vicious warrior surprised his spiritual cousin. The young Tonkawa had wisdom hidden under the scary facade. Potak believed his fearless demeanor allowed his enemies to ignore his wisdom. However, it was a pearl of different wisdom than the medicine man. The shaman knew about the Indian spirit world, and the famous warrior knew about life and death—especially death.

The leathery Indians chuckled. They looked in their twenties, but the medicine man's eyes appeared as ageless as the ocean. As the day came, they sat in the shade of a tree. It was the only tree for miles. They sat there for the entire day and the next night too. Finally, they gathered their meager possessions and removed any sign of their presence. Then, Tuc and Potak seemed to drift across the landscape more like ghosts than mortal men. Suddenly they both drifted into a shadow and didn't reappear. They were swallowed by dark places and vanished without a trace. Only the scent of wild animals lingered in the air.

A LOOK AT BOOK TWO:
RUN FOR YOUR LIFE

They've outrun the law before—but this time, death is riding hard behind.

John Washington—once John Noland—was enslaved and forced to ride with Quantrill's Raiders during the war. He didn't ask for that past, but it won't let go. Now he's wanted for murder, and the men coming for him don't care about justice… they want vengeance.

Jed Coal never chose to be a killer. Drafted into the Confederate Army, he was stolen by Quantrill and forged into a sharpshooter with no way out. But he's loyal to a fault, and he'll stand by John, no matter the cost.

Jodi Goodnight lost her family ranch and her place in the world. Branded an outlaw after defending her own dignity, she's been running ever since. Now she's found a kind of family in Jed and John, but that family is about to be torn apart.

When old war riders like Jesse and Frank James and the Younger brothers return to settle old debts, the fugitives are thrown into a violent whirlwind from Texas to the borderlands. The past is coming fast, and there's only one way to survive: run.

Can they outrun their pasts—or will it finally ride them down for good?

AVAILABLE AUGUST 2025

ABOUT THE AUTHOR

Born in 1886 in Southern Ohio, Ash Lingam grew crops, raised cattle, and doted on the young boy. Ash's family was among the early settlers in pre-Revolutionary America. He has traced his lineage back to around 1746 when his ancestors immigrated from Europe to the aspiring American Colonies.

A retired marketing executive, Ash devotes his spare time to training police dogs and writing novels. He has found his niche in the Western, historical fiction, and adventure genres. With his vast vault of experience, he never runs out of sources for new stories. He has lived in eleven different countries and worked in a total of forty-six to date, Ash has written approximately 130 novels, short stories, and poems. More than one hundred of his eclectic titles help the American frontier come alive for his readers.

https://www.ashlingam.com/

www.ingramcontent.com/pod-product-compliance
Lightning Source LLC
Chambersburg PA
CBHW011436240626
47153CB00011B/3018

* 9 7 8 1 9 6 5 5 9 6 4 9 4 *